Orb Web Tales

Gerald Finlay

First published in Great Britain
by

SRE-F (BOOKS)
Hambleton, Selby, North Yorkshire.

CIP catalogue record for this book is available from the British Library

ISBN: 978-0-9556817-0-7

Cover photograph by Gerald Finlay © 2007

Cover design by Peter J. Merrigan

Dedication

For Shirley and my family

About the Author

Gerald Finlay is a writer of fiction, non-fiction and poetry. He is retired medical engineer, and has been married to Shirley for 46 years. They have two daughters, a son and five grandchildren.

Gerald lives in North Yorkshire with Shirley and Tinker their Yorkshire Terrier.

Contents

Orb Web Tales

The Night Visitor

Lily was the one under discussion, and the discussion was centred on her imaginary friend. Many children if not all have imaginary friends, but Lily's friend seemed to be too real for comfort, and her mum and dad were getting a little worried about it.

Lily was seven, going on eight. She was a bright child doing well at school and had no known problems. She had plenty of friends, was athletic and very musical, playing the piano well. It was relatively recently that her new friend had been visiting during the night. It seemed at first so real, that mum and dad had checked the house security. There was in fact nothing disturbed, and no sign of entry. Harvey the Jack Russell dog, who would normally bark at a feather dropping, had not made a sound, but yet Lily was adamant that her new friend had visited her in the night on a number of occasions.

Trying to find out his identity was proving to be very difficult. It was established he was definitely male, friendly, not posing any kind of threat, and wanting to talk. Lily could not, or would not, relay any more details other than to say his name was Sexton. It was established that Sexton visited about three times a week, and had been doing so for about a month. Her parents had only been made aware of him one week ago.

Lily had complained of a headache one particular morning and her mother had kept her from school. That was the morning that the school bus crashed, and some of the children were injured. It was not until later that evening when they were discussing the accident that Lily told her parents that Sexton had warned her about the crash, and he had told her not to go on the bus. She did in fact not have a headache, but was sure the bus would crash.

Lily's parents decided she should see a doctor and arrangements were made. Dr Blick was a friend of the family. Lily's father was in property and moved in the same circles as the doctor. They had in fact been at the same university, and although studying different subjects, had remained firm friends. The meeting was pre-arranged without Lily being aware. The doctor visited the house as if it was just a friendly visit. Lily's nocturnal visitor was introduced very carefully into the conversation, and Lily was quite happy to discuss him.

When Lily was no longer present the doctor told her parents that he didn't think there was anything to worry about. Lily was nearing the time when her brain and body would be undergoing tremendous change, and he knew of cases where imagination had played many strange tricks. With respect to the school bus crashing, she had obviously convinced herself that she knew about it beforehand. The wondrous workings of a child's mind, was how he described it. However he did suggest that maybe to be on the safe side she should see a consultant psychiatrist friend of his. The appointment was duly arranged. The week before Lily was due to see the consultant her parents told her about the visit. She was told in a casual manner that she would be going with them to see another doctor for some routine tests about medical insurance. Lily didn't seem at all perturbed by this until her father told her it would be the next Thursday.

"We won't be able to go on Thursday Daddy," she said. "That's the day we will be at Granddad's funeral."

Lily's father knew now that there was something seriously wrong with her. His father was a police superintendent; he was also an extremely fit and healthy sixty-year-old. He had in fact only been speaking to him on the phone that morning to arrange a forthcoming outing.

That evening after Lily had gone to bed her parents were having a quiet drink, and discussing their daughter's nightly visitor. The telephone interrupted their conversation. Her mother walked into the hall to answer the phone whilst her father poured them another Tia Maria. When her mother returned to the room a few minutes later, she had her handkerchief up to her face.

"I'm sorry Thomas, that was your brother Adrian on the phone, it's bad news I'm afraid, your father has just had a heart attack and died."

Thomas and his wife were now holding one another and sobbing quietly. If they could have seen through the ceiling above them, they would have seen Lily just starting another conversation with Sexton.

The next morning, Friday, Lily's parents were making their way to Adrian's home. Neither of them said much, but it wouldn't have been difficult to know what they were thinking. They had told Lily about her Granddad that morning before setting out but she didn't react, as they would have expected. She had given her mum and dad a big hug, which once again had produced tears, but strangely for a little girl who could be usually quite emotional she was amazingly calm.

"Will I be able to go to the funeral next Thursday?" were her only words. They told Lily that they didn't know yet when the funeral would be, and that they would see, adding that maybe she was a little young. They had arranged for a neighbour to look after her, and when they were ready to start out, Lily ran to the car and said, "Don't worry about Granddad, he is quite all right. Don't be sad."

As their car pulled into the drive they realised a few other people were there. This was the part they had dreaded. Thomas's brother had lived with their dad since their mother had passed away, and knowing how very close they were to each other, he knew the next few minutes would be quite traumatic. He asked Chloe, Lily's mum, to give him some time before coming in the house herself, and she was more than happy to agree. As Thomas entered the house the friends and relatives, who were present, discreetly stepped aside. Thomas and

Adrian hugged each other, and Thomas quietly asked his brother when the funeral would be. Adrian replied hoarsely, "Tuesday afternoon."

On hearing these words Thomas said with some relief, "Am I pleased to hear that."

Adrian looked puzzled, and Thomas added, "I will explain to you later."

Chloe entered shortly afterwards, and what followed was the usual pattern of small talk and anecdotes. The other visitors soon drifted away, Lily's mum and dad and Adrian were left alone. Thomas then asked about the circumstances of his father death. Adrian explained that their father had just finished his dinner, had poured himself a glass of his favourite tipple, peach schnapps, and sat down to watch the evening news on the television. Shortly after, he heard the glass fall, and when he went to his dad he realised that he was dead. They managed a smile when Adrian added, "At least he drank the Schnapps before he went. He never liked waste."

The couple then related the tale about Lily to Adrian, but were careful to avoid saying anything about her apparent premonition regarding the funeral date. Uncle Adrian and Lily had always been very close and he was obviously very interested in what they had to say, but was not prepared to think there was anything that could not be easily explained. He said that perhaps they should all meet together with Lily and talk about it, but it would have to be after the funeral. After a short time they said goodbye, and the couple left for home.

"I can't tell you how relieved I was when Adrian told me the funeral was on Tuesday," said Thomas as they commenced their drive home.

"Yes, me too," Chloe added. "One bit of good news anyway."

It was the Monday before the funeral; Thomas had been on his computer most of the day catching up on his e-mails, He had just disconnected when the telephone rang. Closing the hall door to drown the noise of Lily practising her piano, he lifted the phone to hear Adrian on the other end.

"Thomas, I have been trying to get you for ages. You have been engaged every time I tried."

"Oh I'm sorry," said Thomas, "I have been on my computer most of the day, but you know my mobile number."

"Your mobile is not switched on," replied Adrian a little coldly.

"Oh blast, I am sorry, I have been in trouble for that before. Sorry old man. I really must get on broadband."

"It's okay Thomas I am a bit touchy, I have had a bad day. The funeral directors called me this morning. There has been a lack of communication between them and the coroner's office. Because Dad's was a sudden death and he was a serving police officer, the regulations say that they have to hold a further enquiry into his death. The fools never arranged it. It's going to delay the funeral I'm afraid. I have managed to reach everyone else to tell them, you were the first on the list, but you have ended up being the last to be told. The only day we could arrange was Thursday."

It was Lily who heard the phone drop and ran into the hall to see what was wrong. Her dad looked at her, took her hand and said quietly, "Lily how did you know your Granddad would die? How did you know his funeral would be on Thursday? Why haven't you been upset about it all?"

Lily looked up at her dad and smiled. "Sexton told me daddy, he is always right. He tells me all sorts of things. He told me not to be sad about Granddad, he told me he was happy, with Grandma. I was pleased about that, not sad."

Lily started to walk out of the hall, then turned and looked over her shoulder as only little girls can do, and said, "I know what's going to happen on Sunday, Daddy."

The phone was still dangling, with the echo of Adrian shouting "Hello" as Lily walked back to the piano to continue practising Beethoven's Ode to Joy.

The funeral came and went, as funerals do. Lily's prediction for the Sunday before also came true. But I cannot elaborate on this at the moment. Adrian was as good as his word, and an informal post funeral meeting was arranged which would give another opportunity to talk to Lily, and for Adrian to assess things. Lily was perfectly co-operative as indeed she always was; Sexton was still visiting, and telling her things. Her schooling and music were also progressing very well, it was clear that Lily's nocturnal experiences were not affecting her abnormally in any way. Nothing new was gleaned from this meeting apart from a couple more predictions from Lily via Sexton. Adrian suggested that the cancelled appointment with the consultant should be rearranged, and he expressed a desire to be there. There was no objection to this and the appointment was duly arranged.

Thomas and Chloe were talking with the consultant for about thirty minutes before Lily and Adrian were called in. Mr Glass, the consultant, then told Lily what he knew about Sexton, and asked her if she would mind talking about his visits to her. Lily was quite happy to talk. She was fully aware by now of the reason for her visit. The consultant was very careful in his questioning, and also surprised by the answers. He made some attempts to trick Lily, but was unable to do so.

Whilst having a quiet word with Thomas after he had examined Lily, Mr Glass confessed to being puzzled. He could find no medical reason to explain things, indeed he expressed the opinion that Lilly was a perfectly normal little girl, but obviously forward for her years. His suggestion was that a small camera should be fitted in Lily's room. His thoughts were that it would maybe be possible to see whether she was just dreaming, or if …. Nobody cared to venture what the "if" might be. Lily was asked about this, it was not of course the thing to do, to spy on a young girl. After some discussion Lily said it was okay, as long it was not switched on until she was in bed, and switched off before she got up. She was promised this would be the case, and the camera was installed. It was programmed to switch on at eleven pm, and off at six am – plenty of safety margins for Lily. The day after the camera was first put into use, Thomas and Chloe were eager to view the results. At about one in the morning Lily became restless, then sat up in bed and said in a clear voice, "Hello Sexton!"

The camera was wide angled, and clearly there was nobody else in the room. Lily was then going through the motions of a conversation but not actually speaking; her silent exchange lasted about ten minutes, then she lay back down and went back to sleep. She did not wake until her normal time.

That evening after tea Lily sat with her mum and dad to discuss the camera results. She was adamant Sexton was present and that she had spoken to him, and to prove it she would tell them what was going to happen in two days. The camera check lasted one week; the predictions again came true.

A further meeting was arranged to discuss a course of action. Those present at the next meeting were Dr Blick, Mr Glass, mum and dad, and a representative from the church where Lily took organ lessons. Adrian was also present, and one other important person. I have to tell you that apart from the incident with the school bus, and granddad's funeral, none of Lily's predictions have been made public. It was clear from the beginning that much benefit, financial and otherwise, could have been made from them. It was unanimously agreed by all present that details would not be released. The implications of going public, although very tempting, were enormous. Nothing further was gleaned from the second meeting.

Lily's meetings with Sexton continued until she was about ten and a half. On the night when Lily changed from being a girl to becoming a young lady her visits from Sexton ended. All Lily's predictions have been carefully documented and verified. She always said that it would never be possible to change the future, Sexton had told her, and that she had no idea why he had picked her for his visits.

Lily grew up a lovely lady, a brilliant academic, and a fine musician. She graduated from Oxford with a double first, Summa cum Laude. She is now a consultant obstetrician and a professor of child psychiatry. She also holds a PhD in music, and is in demand as a pianist and organist. It has been agreed that the details Lily acquired whilst being visited by Sexton will not be made public until after her death. I can tell you however that amazingly all her many predictions have been correct – and that there is still one outstanding!

Lily does not and has not given any predictions since the night of her transition from child to young lady. I can tell you however that even now she does make some uncanny prophesies from time to time. I am not, because of constraints, allowed to reveal the date or place of this account, other than to say – it was in the 20th century, and in England.

By the way, Lily is now both a mother and grandmother. You may want to ask what my qualifications are for writing this story with such authority. Well maybe I should explain. Lily and I have been married forty-six years this year.

If you are wondering if this story is true the answer is clear within the text.

Floating

I first encountered Lenny at the bottom of Dead Man's Hill. I am not sure where that name came from, but I think it was a route taken to bury folks who were killed on the nearby dam construction, many years ago. It was a glorious day and I was leisurely strolling along, taking in the beautiful scenery and listening to the birds, when I became aware of someone walking down a track towards the one I was on. He seemed to have a strange gait, as if limping. Where the tracks joined we met. He introduced himself as Lenny; it was clear from the start that he had a problem. He was a very friendly guy of about forty and could probably be described in a polite way as being slow, not physically you understand, but clearly his way of walking was connected to his problem. He spoke very clearly and slowly and tried to avoid any long words, which if attempted usually came out wrong. Lenny was heading for Loftgill, he apparently lived there. By coincidence that was where I was spending the next few nights, using it as a starting off point for my walks. It was time for lunch, I asked Lenny if he wanted to stop and eat with me and he seemed happy to do so. We picked a nice spot overlooking the dam at the end of the large reservoir, and sat down on the heather to share our soup and sandwiches.

"You are nice, not many people talk to me in the village, they think I am silly because I do not talk like them, I have to think before I talk you see. I go to our church, they let me give the books out before the service; but not many people talk to me there either. They look at me because I walk funny, but I bet I can walk further than them."

"I bet you can Lenny, you are obviously a very fit man. I also go to church and not many people talk to me either, so don't let that worry you. Have you lived in Loftgill long? Do you have family there?"

"I have lived there all my life I think, but I do not remember things very well. I live on my own, but some people help me. I have a friend, she is Samantha, she is helping with my book."

"Are you writing a book then?" I enquired.

"No I cannot write much; I can write my name though. Sam is helping me to read a book."

"Oh that is excellent Lenny, reading is super, you are lucky having someone to help you. What is the book about?"

"It is about floating."

"Floating? Oh, that sounds interesting," I replied, trying to imagine what floating was. Lenny helped me to finish my coffee, and we set off over the moors to Loftgill.

After a nice bath and a relaxing half-hour with the morning paper, I made my way down to the bar for a little drink before my evening meal. My new friend had gone off to his home; I had arranged to meet him in the morning to go on one of his favourite walks. I found that I got on very well with Lenny, and his slight problem was certainly no problem to me. Whilst I was at the bar I heard someone say "Hello Samantha". I turned around to see a lady walking out of the hotel past a couple who were sat beside the door. Could this be Lenny's Samantha? I strolled over.

"Excuse me for interrupting you, but I just heard that lady call you Samantha. Are you by any chance the Samantha who helps Lenny?"

"I certainly am the same," said the lady smiling.

"I hope you don't think me rude, but could I speak to you for a few minutes?" I explained briefly about meeting Lenny on the moor.

"No problem, sit down and join us. This is my husband Alec." I introduced myself, and called the waiter over to order some drinks before I sat down.

"Lenny said you were helping him with a book about floating."

Samantha laughed. "Oh, he has told you about that has he? And you would like to know where I fit in?"

"Well I am just curious," I said.

"Okay, let me explain. About six months ago Lenny came into the Library where I work, well actually I am the only one who works there ...." She grinned. "He went to the children's section where he always picks his books from, he doesn't read very well and he likes lots of pictures. What do you think he picked? The only book in the children's section that had been put back in the wrong place, a book about levitation."

"Levitation? – Floating! Oh, I am beginning to see," I said.

"Yes," said Samantha, smiling again. "Lenny can't say levitation, but he saw some pictures in the book, and said the people were floating. There was no way I could get the book from him, so I let him take it out. Unfortunately it didn't end there. As expected, Lenny couldn't read the book and returned to ask if I would help. Well, as you can imagine we are not too busy here, so I decided to help him read it. I used the library's computer, and activated the character recognition programme. I then altered all the words Lenny couldn't read to easy words, and scanned it out for him. It took me about three weeks to do it, but Lenny can read it now. He tells everyone about his 'floating' book."

"What exactly is wrong with Lenny then?" I enquired.

"We're not sure," said Alec. "I have known him the longest. I think it was some congenital problem to start with, then some family problem. He seems to have been here forever. I am the church organist, and he often comes to sit with me when I am practising, he loves music."

Shortly afterwards I left Samantha and Alec, and went through to the dining room. That night when in bed, my mind went back many years to my days in the Royal Air Force. There was this guy called Corporal Walls, he served behind the bar in our mess. Walls was a big guy, probably about 15 stone. I don't know how it started, but someone told us it was possible to lift a large person with two fingers. Of course everyone scoffed, but the smiles were quickly wiped of our faces. I thought it was a trick until it came to my turn. Corporal Walls was seated in his chair. One of my friends stood at one side of the chair, I stood at the other. He was instructed to put both hands on his head. I then put my hands on his, then my friend put his hands on mine. Walls was then told to pull down as hard as he could, and we had to push down as hard as we could. This lasted about thirty seconds. We had previously been told that when we were given the signal, we should remove our hands. The corporal would place his hands on his shoulders, with his elbows down, and we should then place our index fingers under his elbows, one at each side of course. We were then told to lift. Walls came out of the chair without any effort. We held him there for at least ten seconds then slowly lowered him, with just two fingers, into his chair. Nobody believed it until they tried, then they believed.

I awoke nice and early the next morning looking forward to my day on the moors with Lenny. He was waiting for me outside my hotel at nine on the dot, and wanted to take me to the old lead mines. I had been there a number of times, but I didn't tell him this, I knew though that we were in for a difficult hike, the lead mines where at least four miles of hard climbing. I asked Lenny what he did the previous evening, he replied that he had been floating.

"Do you mean that you were reading your book? Samantha told me how she had helped you. I met her last night at my hotel."

"Yes I was reading my book. Sam did it so I could read the words, Sam is nice. I can float now."

"What do you mean you can float now, Lenny?" I enquired.

"Well ever since Sam made the words so that I could read them I have been trying to float, it looks so nice, I did it last night. What are you having for lunch?"

Well whatever Lenny did last night, it certainly hadn't affected him, and lunch seemed more important than anything else did. We eventually arrived at the lead mines and sat down to have a drink and take in the glorious views.

"Lenny, when you said you were floating last night, what did you do?"

"Oh, that. Do you want me to show you?"

"Well yes, I would be interested to see."

"Okay then, I will try."

Lenny sat down on one of the slabs left over from the mines, crossed his legs and arms, and closed his eyes. After about five minutes nothing had happened, and I felt sure he was in some kind of dream imagining himself to be floating. Then the most extraordinary thing happened, he started to lift from the ground, only very slightly at first. I thought he was lifting himself, but after a few seconds there was light beneath him. He rose about eight inches, then opened his eyes. Then he smiled and slowly returned to the ground.

"I told you I could float." I was speechless and open mouthed. What I had just witnessed was impossible, but I had just seen it.

Two days later Lenny died in his sleep. He had a heart condition that the doctors knew about. It seems that he had done well to last so long. I dare not say anything to anyone about what I had seen, even Samantha and Alec. The funeral was organised a couple of days later so I was able to go. I asked Alec if any particular music had been picked, to play in church. Apparently it hadn't, it had been left to him.

"Would you play something for me, Alec? I think Lenny would have liked it."

"Yes, no problem," Alec replied. "As long as I know it."

"It's that pop song of a few years ago, 'He ain't heavy, he's my brother'."

"Oh, that one? No problem, I love it. I have the music at home on my keyboard, I will be delighted to play it."

Lenny had told me he hadn't many friends, but the church was packed to the door on the day of the funeral. As the coffin was carried in Alec started to play "He ain't heavy" like I have never heard it before. I swear there wasn't a dry eye in the church. Everyone in the village had contributed to get Lenny a lovely spot in the churchyard looking out over the moors. That was one walking holiday that ended on a sad note. I did finish the holiday, but could not get what I had seen out of my mind.

Addendum.

After my holiday I went into our university library, and did some reading on levitation. There have been cases of levitation documented, but these have all been associated with spiritualism, and have only been documented in religious references. However I did read an article by an eminent scientist who stated: *Levitation could never be performed by anyone studying it. It could never be performed by anyone doubting it. An academic could never perform it. There is no doubt in my mind however that given the right circumstances and instruction, levitation could be performed by a child.*

Some months later I returned to Loftgill and told Samantha and Alec the full story. As expected it soon got round the village. Lenny now has celebrity status. So if you are ever in North Yorkshire why not call in at Loftgill churchyard and pay your respects to Lenny. If you have trouble finding Loftgill just ask for the "floating" village. That's how it is now affectionately called – and everyone knows it.

Dissecting the Human Brain

I have been told many times that I was brainless, or brain dead, so I decided to have a closer look and see if my accusers were correct. My first conclusion was that if I was brain dead then I wouldn't feel any pain when I investigated, the same applies to being brainless of course. I stood with a large mirror in front, and one behind, and made a large incision across my cranium. I made a large one just in case there was anything there.

Well there was certainly something there, and obviously now I had to proceed with caution. To dissect I had to remove first. I knew that if I damaged my medulla oblongata, my respiration, heartbeat, strength and blood pressure would be in deep trouble. I had obviously to take great care of the brain stem! I removed and dissected the cerebellum first. This controls muscular and limb movement; but I am sure that you know this. I proceeded very slowly. Obviously I had to be able to put it back together later.

Next was the cerebrum, all sorts of things happened then; I started to cry when I remembered all the bad behaviour that I thought I had might have been involved in. It was a good job that I had two bits of cerebrum – because one of them fell on the floor, and I couldn't remember what it looked like, or where it had gone. I then decided to investigate the synapses and neurotransmitters to see if I could find out why, when I told myself to do something, I usually did it wrong, tripped up, or got things the wrong way round.

By now I was feeling extremely confident, and decided to risk it and go for the cerebral cortex. This of course is the real grey matter, and in higher mammals, (don't know if that includes me, I am 5ft11ins) it develops folds in unassigned areas. These folds represent intelligence, personality, and higher mental faculties. I didn't expect to find much here, and I was right – even though I had a good poke round.

I then dissected the two small areas at the left side of the brain that I knew were to do with languages. When I opened up, I found all these French, Spanish, and German words all mixed up together. No wonder I always had trouble speaking them. The English words were in a different place and were all very short. There wasn't a great deal of them either I'm afraid!

Next I encountered the Brocas's area (speech) this didn't seem to have much inside which probably explains why, when I try to say anything, it usually comes out total rubbish. Wernicke's section was my ultimate encounter, this as you are no doubt all aware is the bit to do with comprehension of the spoken and written word. Needless to say after scratching around in here for some time I came across nothing of interest at all.

I then found I had a right mess on my hands, but nevertheless I set about trying to put it all back together. It took me a few hours – I was working through a mirror remember. It didn't take me too long though, to realise that I must have put it all back in the wrong way round; the reason being, when I try to lift my left arm, my right one comes up, and when I try to walk with my left foot first, my right leg leaps out.

Mais allus ist richtig avec mio avec el parabla Espania und das Francais habla el deautch ich denka merci. – Did I get that right?

I of course have one big advantage now, because if anybody attempts that frontal lobotomy that I have been threatened with on numerous occasions, I will bet my bottom dollar they go in at the wrong place.

A Good Day for a Hunt

Nathan Brock was a nasty man; nobody would argue with that. He was rich, but only through his family; he had never had a real job. His family owned hundreds of acres of countryside, and since his father's death, he was I suppose, the Lord of the Manor. He gave his workers a hard time, paid them little, and expected them to fawn round him in the local, laughing at his unfunny jokes. They always did, but what they said behind his back was something else.

Young Tanya was in hospital, it was not known if she would recover. John, her brother, and Tim her boyfriend had hardly left her side since she had received her injuries. On the day of the incident, Cragside was having one of its quite frequent hunts. Not many people liked the hunt locally, and most participants came in from surrounding areas. Opposition to the hunt was strong, and mostly from locals who had placards. These people milled around and let their feelings about hunting be known, but only in a peaceful way. John, Tim and Tanya were part of the protesters.

Nathan Brock as you would probably have guessed, was the hunt master, lording it about in his fancy garb, and quite obviously feeling the effects of drink. He was currently drinking port wine from a pewter tankard. It was Tanya who approached Brock and held her placard up to him. It read, "Stop this disgusting hunting". He had swung round with his tankard and smashed Tanya just above the temple. She crumpled to the floor.

When the police came to arrest Brock for assault later that day, he claimed he had acted in self defence and that Tanya had struck him with the placard. He had a large weal on his cheek to prove it. He had in fact continued with the hunt, not even waiting for the ambulance to arrive. No one had seen any mark on his face; no one had seen him struck. It was only after he realised he could be in trouble and had seen his solicitor that the mark appeared. His subsequent answer was that it took some time for the mark to show. The local magistrates dismissed the case as self defence; this was fully expected in the village. Brock walked free, with not one word of remorse; Tanya was fighting for her life.

Tanya had known Tim for about a year; they were planning to get married. Tim had been at university with John, and was now a Chemist. John was a junior general practitioner. Tanya taught at the local junior school, was in the church choir and was loved and respected throughout the village. She lived with her brother in the house that had been their parents'. Tim lived a few miles away at Moston, the next village.

Brock was going on holiday to America, the entire village knew and was glad. The only reason he was tolerated was because he gave employment to locals who would otherwise be out of work. They could of course draw unemployment benefit which would probably have been as much money, but these were proud people and needed to work for their keep.

"This could be our best opportunity Tim," said John, "are you sure you can go through with it?"

"You just watch me mate, you just watch."

It had been planned very carefully, ever since Tanya had received her injury in fact. They had been waiting for a suitable time, and this seemed to be it.

"Well, Brock leaves on Wednesday at five thirty am. He is driving himself to Manchester airport, to catch a plane at ten thirty, and planning to stay a month. It will be getting light at that time, it should just be just right," replied John.

"You seem to have got it well sussed out," said Tim.

"Well there is some advantage to being the local doctor you know," grinned John, "people tell you things; but don't forget your contribution Tim, that should clinch it for us."

It was six weeks since the incident. Tanya was making a little progress; she was suffering from amnesia, caused by the head fracture. She also had lost her sense of smell. Having only been fully conscious a few days, it was not known whether she would ever regain her full faculties, or indeed be able to walk again. Her room was always full of beautiful flowers and cards sent by the villagers.

The clock said four thirty. It was Thursday morning. Tim had just picked John up in his Land Rover; he also had a trailer on the back. They set off quietly to the lane end that came down from Brock Manor. At about five Nathan Brock was driving down the track from the manor to the road; he didn't have a care in the world, and was looking forward to his holiday. John and Tim heard him approaching; they had parked their Land Rover across the exit to the track; Nathan Brock got out of his car and walked up to the Land Rover.

"What the bloody hell is going on here? Move this damn thing, I have to catch a plane at Manchester."

"Sorry Brock but you won't be catching a plane today, we have something else in mind for you," said John emerging from behind the Land Rover.

"What's that suppose to mean you bloody fool? Get this car moved or else!"

Tim had opened the back of his trailer and two massive Alsatian dogs were brought out.

"Just stay calm Brock, or we will turn the dogs on you now," said Tim, who was restraining the two dogs on stout leashes.

"I am glad to see you have trainers on Nathan, you are going to need them, we have in mind for you a little run" said John, with just a faint smile. Brock had done a bit of fell running, John and Tim had too, they had in fact competed in the same events. They were all about the same level which had made this morning's exercise easier to plan.

"What do you mean run? Come on you two, you know I have a plane to catch, enough of this silliness," said Brock in a quieter voice – with just a hint of concern.

"Don't say anything else Brock, just listen very closely to what I say," replied John. "You love to hunt, and delight in the chase and slaughter of creatures; you now are going to be the hunted. The difference will be that you will have a chance, which your prey never has. Take your clothes off apart from your underclothes and trainers."

Brock made to object until Tim eased nearer with the two growling dogs; he then complied. He had on a pair of Boxer shorts, a thin singlet and his trainers; for all the world dressed for a morning run. John then moved Brock's car into one of the nearby barns that had been selected earlier, he also moved the Land Rover and trailer behind the wall of the drive; but not before removing two already saddled horses from the trailer. Brock was now looking round anxiously, but was pinned against the wall by Tim with the dogs.

"Okay Brock, listen very carefully, this is your cross-country run for today. You will run from here down to Black Bog bottom, across the stream, through Buxted woods and up the slope to Oakridge. If you make it to Oakridge you have won; you can then jog down to Moston. We will not chase you there. To the top of Oakridge from here is about six miles; given the terrain and your ability we reckon you can do it in forty-two minutes. We have been fair in calculating your start, and have made allowances for the dogs chasing your scent. You should make it okay, but you just will not know. If you are caught, the dogs will have you to themselves for a while before we arrive. You are going to experience what it is like to be hunted."

"You will never get away with this," said a now clearly agitated Brock.

"Oh, why is that?" replied Tim. "If you make Oakridge before us we just turn round and ride away. If you don't – well we have thought about that also."

"Nobody ever goes through Black bog bottom, it's too dangerous," croaked Block.

"Only at certain times," said John. "It's quite safe at the moment if you run, quite dry actually. I have run this route a number of times recently, don't worry Black Bog is not your problem. The bottle please Tim."

Tim produced a bottle and unscrewed the top. The dogs immediately became restless. Tim passed the bottle under the dog's noses, and then approached Brock.

"Stick your right leg out, the dogs need a scent." Brock had no option; the liquid was poured on his leg.

"Now the left arm." Liquid was then poured on his left forearm.

"Now listen carefully," said John. "You should be able to do this okay, but don't waste any time, it will be close. Do not deviate, you know the quickest way, stick to it. If you decide to go to the right or left the dogs will catch you long before you reach safety, they will not lose the scent. Now you are about to experience terror. Set your stop watch, you have forty-two minutes to make Oakridge."

John and Tim also set their watches. Brock set off at a fast pace for Black Bog bottom. He kept glancing at his watch. *Going okay so far – keep calm, should do this okay, keep calm. Don't hear the dogs, must have a good start. They are bloody having me on, the swines, they couldn't do this to me; can't risk it though, must keep going. Plenty of time, should still make the airport okay. Hope Black Bottom is fairly dry, people have been lost in that bog and never been found! I will see them pay for this – who do they bloody well think they are? I'll bloody show them, they'll find out who is boss around here. Ah Black Bog coming up, doing okay; still feeling good. The stream – shall I stop to try to rinse the scent off, should be okay for a minute, no sound of the dogs. Bloody hell! The scent is just as strong, what have they used? I must have lost two minutes, what a bloody fool.*

Brock was now experiencing the first taste of terror, he made his first mistake stopping at the stream, and he was now stumbling over obstacles instead of clearing them. John and Tim were trotting steadily in pursuit; the dogs still in check.

"If I guessed right Brock will have stopped at the stream to try to wash the scent off," said John. "He will be rattled by now, know he has lost time; but will still feel confident though because he can't hear the dogs."

Tim looked at his watch, "Okay dogs – it is hunting time." He leaned over and unhitched the leashes and the two dogs took off like lightning. "I hope he isn't expecting to hear them," said Tim smiling, and knowing full well that German Shepherd dogs never make a sound when hunting.

I can't go any faster, but I still can't hear the dogs. I bet they are not chasing me at all. Soon be through the woods, should be easier then. Those two morons could be at home now bloody laughing at me. I could stop and walk back, that would show them they hadn't fooled me, but what if they are still after me; must keep going. I could stop and pick up a rock or a stick, I would lose more time though; can't risk it, best keep on, not too far now – still can't hear the dogs. Oakridge up there, can see it now, four hundred bloody yards and I am home safe. Slowing now; this hill is a killer – come on legs, come on. Was that the dogs I heard? No don't think so; might have been though. God help me. Our father who art in heaven – oh bloody hell, come on legs: Lord have mercy. Nearly there now.

Nathan Brock was about two hundred yards from Oakridge when he felt the excruciating pain in his right calf; a second later he felt a similar pain in his left arm. The dogs had him!

It was about ten seconds before John and Tim rode up, but by then Brock was badly mauled.

"Okay dogs, enough. Here!" The dogs immediately came to Tim's side and sat down. Brock was on his back, clearly terrified.

"Didn't quite make it Nathan then? What bad luck. Still you didn't do too badly, bet you stopped at the stream, told you not to. How does it feel to be hunted?"

"You bloody barbarians, get me some help quickly I am in agony."

"Agony? You don't know what agony is. What do think the poor fox feels when you ride out with your moronic acolytes, and all those screaming dogs? You chase the poor things until they drop exhausted, then let the dogs rip them apart. If the fox outruns you and goes to earth, do you say enough, the fox deserves to live? Do you bloody hell – you dig the terrified creature out of his earth and throw him to the dogs."

"Yes but they are only foxes," groaned Brock.

"You heartless thug," replied John, "they are God's creatures – mammals like you and I, warm blooded with families; they feel the same terror and pain as you and I, and Tanya does. Why did you nearly kill the girl? We know she never touched you, we know what your crooked solicitor put you up to, and we know the chief magistrate was a crony of yours. Well Brock, the truth now or we release the dogs again."

"Alright, alright," spluttered Brock, now visibly shaking. "It's true she didn't touch me, but I thought she was going to; I was annoyed at the demonstrators, they are a bloody nuisance; I mean why don't they leave us alone?"

"You just rode away," Tim interrupted very quietly, "never stopped to see how she was, never enquired about her at the hospital – you just didn't care. You nearly killed her, she is my fiancée."

"Okay okay I am sorry, I will give up hunting; I will send some flowers, just get me some medical help quickly."

"We are letting you off lightly Brock, but you don't deserve it. I will give you something for the pain. Tim, the bottle please." Tim handed the bottle to John, who unscrewed the stopper and sprinkled the liquid into Brock's arm and leg wounds. Brock screamed in agony. John then said, "Okay Nathan my friend, you may as well have the rest of this; we will not be needing it again." John then emptied the rest of the bottle down the front of Brock. "Something for you to smell when we go."

The dogs were now noticeably restless. Tim shouted at them, "Be still dogs!" John and Tim then turned and rode away.

"You can't leave me here like this, you can't leave me like this, for God's sake have you no pity?" shouted Brock. The two riders stopped.

"He is right Tim, you know we cannot leave him like that."

"Yes I know," said Tim, "what on earth are we thinking of, we certainly cannot leave him like that." Without another word Tim and John reached down and unfastened the dogs. The two dogs raced back to Brock!

Tim and John cantered down the hill. The screams lasted for about thirty seconds, then there was silence; apart from the padding of hooves: As the two riders exited Buxted woods and were approaching Black Bog bottom the two dogs caught them up. They dismounted, took the dogs to the stream and washed them thoroughly. They then cantered back to where the hunt had started. It was all over in sixty-five minutes.

The horses were quickly loaded in the trailer, followed by the dogs. John was dropped off just outside the village about two hundred yards from home. Tim took the back, single-track road to Moston, which took him to his property without passing any other dwellings. He quickly had the horses stabled, then showered and changed. He still had time to have a bite to eat before setting off in his sports car for Darrogate. He was in no hurry now. Tim stopped at the old lead mine just off the main road, making sure no-one was about, he dropped the bottle down the deep shaft, He knew it would fragment, and any residue would just evaporate.

The Pharmaceutical Centre where Tim was a research chemist soon came into view. Everything had gone like clockwork. Back at Tim's house the two Alsatians were fast asleep in the large compound. Things continued as normal in the village, Brock would not be missed for four weeks or maybe five. It was not unusual for him to extend his time away without informing anyone. Nobody had said anything to either John or Tim in Cragside, or Moston, other than normal village talk.

Heavy rain had fallen over the last week, and they knew that any tracks that had been made by horses or dogs would have long since been eliminated. John had walked down to Black Bog bottom it was now totally impassable, no one would be able to cross there for months. There was now no access to Buxted woods. Tim knew that Brock wouldn't be lonely on Oakridge, the powerful substance he had worked on at the pharmaceutical plant, would attract every living thing for miles around – no Brock certainly would not be lonely.

It was two fell walkers who made the discovery five weeks later. In a particularly bad rain storm they had misread their map and had taken the unused Oakridge route, instead of the lower Moston track. They soon realised their error when the track petered out, but not before they came across the remains. At first they thought it to be an animal, as bones were scattered about, but when they found the skull, they knew it was no animal. Brock it seemed had at last been found.

Inspector Dobson from Darrogate Police was put in charge of the case. It was Inspector Dobson who had investigated the assault on Tanya. Both John and Tim knew him. Because of the nature of the case, Dobson was to be supported by members of the forensic department. Oakridge was cordoned off, not that anyone ever went there. It had a large screen round the area were the remains were found, though the people behind the screen didn't know at that time who they had found. Cragside and Moston were checked first for missing people, and it was soon found that Nathan Brock was overdue from his visit to America, and later that he was never actually booked onto his flight at Manchester.

The skull was taken away and dental checks made; it was soon established that it was indeed Brock. The forensic team were in trouble from the start, there was very little, well in fact nothing, for them to do forensic work with. Two chewed Puma running shoes and some bits of fabric were all they found. After two days the remains had been removed and the covers were taken down. Inspector Dobson was seen about Cragside and Moston over the next few days, but did not speak to John or Tim. The remains from Oakridge were sent for post mortem examination, and the date of the coroner's inquest fixed.

John was present at the inquest as a medical observer; he sat well to the back. The bailiff called the court to order, and the coroner asked for the forensic report. The spokesman for the forensic team told the court that after detailed and thorough examination of both the deceased and the area involved, there was nothing found at all to help with identifying the cause of death. The post mortem in fact was no help. The only injuries found had occurred after death, this was damage to bone. There was nothing to indicate any foul play. The coroner thanked the forensic spokesman. Inspector Dobson was then asked for his report.

"Sir this seems at first a strange case. Nathan Brock was disliked by everybody I spoke to in Cragside where he lived. You will know that he was the Lord of the Manor."

"Yes, yes, I did know that"

"Of course sir, I'm sorry. He apparently was on his way to Manchester to catch a plane to America; he was going on holiday sir. For some reason he decided to go for a run before leaving for the plane. No one will ever know why he chose that time to go, but he was in fact known to be a pretty good fell runner. I understand from speaking to some runners from the local club, that runners can be quite eccentric and in fact sometimes do very strange things." There was an outbreak of laughter at this remark, and the bailiff had to ask for silence.

"Yes, yes Dobson, I am well aware of the eccentricity of runners, please continue."

"Well sir, that is the only reason I can suggest why he took himself running before going to catch his plane. Maybe he thought a little exercise before the long plane trip …."

"Yes, quite Dobson," interrupted the coroner. "But what can you tell me about the circumstances of his death?"

"Sir it is my opinion that Brock took himself for an early morning run, got into some difficulty while ascending Oakridge, maybe a heart attack but whatever the cause he was clearly unable to move. Sir, do you want the details out loud?" said Dobson quietly whilst looking around the court. "You already have them in writing."

"This is an open court Dobson, the details please."

"Sir, all that was left of the body was an incomplete skeleton. The only flesh was a little on the skull under the remaining hair." Dobson cleared his throat at this point, then added, "It seems clear to me that Brock was eaten by a family of foxes. The foxes were helped of course by other small animals; and undoubtedly by the many birds round these parts that feed on such remains. In short sir, the body was picked clean. There is absolutely nothing to indicate any foul play."

"Thank you Dobson, this court is adjourned until two-thirty, I will give my verdict then."

The coroner returned punctually at two thirty and immediately started to read his report.

"I wish to thank the forensic team. This cannot have been a nice job for you. I fully understand the nature of your report. Inspector Dobson, your involvement must have been equally difficult, you have given me a concise description of events, I am sure no one could have done better. I am basing my verdict on your report. Thank you also Dobson for your concern about the court.

"It is my opinion that Nathan Brock for reasons only known to him, decided to go for an early morning run. Something that we do not know occurred on that run, which brought about his death. We have to hope that his body was not attacked until after his death. I agree that foxes probably ate him. That is paradoxical in some way. I understand he was the local hunt master. The verdict of this court then is that Nathan Brock died by misadventure. This case is closed."

The service for Brock took place at Cragside church one week after the inquest. Apart from the vicar and choir and a few members of Brock's employ who obviously found it their duty to attend, there was not many in church. John could not attend because of his medical rounds. Tim did not attend because – well he just didn't know Brock well enough. The obligatory few elderly people who never missed a funeral were of course present. Inspector Dobson was also there, and one other person, a total stranger. The vicar stood up and said, "We are not here to be sad today." Everyone seemed to agree with that. "We are here to give thanks for Nathan Brock's life." Everybody seemed to disagree with that. Nevertheless the congregation went on to sing *All Things Bright and Beautiful* and *The Day Thou Gavest Lord Is Ended* with gusto. After the service Inspector Dobson was seen talking to the vicar and the stranger. The stranger was an extremely attractive young woman of about thirty. The vicar and this young woman were the only two people to accompany Brock on his last ride to the crematorium at Darrogate.

Lorna Lampton was not unduly perturbed by Nathan Brock's death. She had had nothing in common with him whatsoever and strongly disliked his way of life. She remembered him as a very selfish and arrogant person. It was only because she was family that she felt obliged to attend his funeral. In fact Lorna was the only family. Brock's parents were both dead; he had been an only child. Lorna's Father was Nathan's father's brother; her parents were both now deceased. Lorna was Nathan's only cousin, and it seemed the nearest relative. She would then inherit the estate and become the Lady of the Manor of Cragside.

Lorna was a veterinary surgeon and had a partnership in Leeds. She had always wanted a country practice, and over the next few weeks spent quite a lot of time about the village, Leeds being only forty miles away. The Vicar had invited Lorna and a few other locals including John to dinner to discuss her ideas. John had in fact met Lorna earlier when she had attended his surgery to ask about registering with him. He had already told her about Tanya and the circumstances of her injuries. Lorna was deeply distressed, and in fact had been to Darrogate hospital to meet Tanya. They had got on well together; Lorna hated hunting also.

Lorna had in mind that the manor could be turned into three separate parts: a country veterinary practice that would treat domestic and farm animals (the nearest vets were in Darrogate, a local vet would be good news for all the locals); an equestrian centre, for tuition in horse riding and cross-country rides, and an outdoor pursuit centre for young people, there being plenty of scope for climbing, caving and water sport activity locally. The manor was big enough to accommodate these activities; Lorna had no desire to live there. These ideas were welcome with much interest, they would in fact increase the local job opportunities, and bring more visitors; excellent news for the village indeed. Lorna made it quite clear she would have nothing to do with hunting, and expressed her hope that the village would cease any connection with hunts.

John and Lorna had been seen together on a few occasions dining together in the village hotel where she stayed whilst visiting Cragside.

John and Tim met occasionally, but not frequently. They did live in different villages and both had busy lives. They did however meet up some times at the hospital where they both visited as much as possible. Tanya was making good progress; she was just recovering from neurosurgery. The swelling had only just reduced enough for this to be done. John knew the surgeon, and had been assured that Tanya would make a near full recovery. John and Tim were both on a high at this news. It was when they were leaving the hospital for the car park one day that they bumped into Inspector Dobson; nothing unusual here, Dobson had been a frequent visitor to Tanya since his involvement with her case. However both John and Tim were a little shocked at what happened next.

"Ah gentlemen I have been wanting to talk to you two together, this seems like a good time, can you spare a few minutes? My car is just over here."

They all walked back to Inspector Dobson's car.

"There are a few things I want to talk to you two about, regarding Brock's unfortunate demise. There are four things actually – they have been bothering me I wondered if you two could help at all?"

"Well of course if we can inspector, but I thought that was all over and done with," said John. John and Tim tried to suppress their sidewards glance at each other but were unable to do so, while still trying not to show any concern.

"Yes indeed, the inquest verdict was clear; however if evidence comes to light that could affect the case …. Inquests can be re-opened, it doesn't happen very often though I have to say." John and Tim tried to make themselves comfortable in the car.

"Firstly then, on that fateful morning; why do you think Brock left his car in the barn at the bottom of his drive and closed the door, doesn't make sense does it? If he intended to drive himself to Manchester, and have a run first, surely he would have started his run from the Manor. If he was going in a taxi to the airport, his car would have been in his garage at the manor. Not in the barn. Very strange, gentlemen, don't you think?

"Second, why the bloody hell would he go for a run at all? He was not an idiot, he would have known full well that starting a run at five – let's say forty minutes to Cragside, then forty minute back, that would be good running for anyone, total time, one hour twenty minutes. He would have needed to shower and change, at least another thirty minutes. Total now nearly two hours. Are you beginning to see where I am leading gentlemen?"

Tim and John remained silent.

"Time now about seven, he then had to drive to Manchester airport. Don't forget heavy morning traffic, and the notorious hold ups going round Manchester. Check in at airport is at least two hours before flight time. Flight time ten-thirty. He would not have had enough time to get from here to the airport. Now if he had set off at about five, as I suspect he intended; he would have missed all the early traffic, and done it in two and a quarter hours easily, arriving at the airport at about the right time. It seems clear to me the Brock never intended to go running that morning."

John and Tim were now looking a little worried.

"Thirdly then, why would Brock go anywhere near Black Bog bottom? Especially on his own, that doesn't make sense. He would know full well how dangerous it is, even in dry weather. Only a complete idiot would risk that, and Brock although a nasty person was not an idiot; anyway there are far better runs he could have done from the manor. It just doesn't make any sense."

Dobson was watching John and Tim closely all the time he was talking.

"Now the last point gentlemen. When we found the remains, we found a pair of trainers. Okay, this would imply he could have been running. We also found some pieces of fabric attached to the remains. Forensic for some reason did not think this significant, no doubt they thought it part of his running gear. I took some samples and had them analysed. The material was fabric that would be used for underclothing! I was assured that garments made for running are made of totally different material. Brock was clearly running in his underclothes. Just doesn't make sense gentlemen does it?"

John was the first to react. "Well Inspector that certainly sounds very interesting, and I can well understand you being a bit puzzled. If it was some medical matter you were asking me about, perhaps I could help you; but I'm afraid detective work is just not my scene."

Tim then joined in. "Like John said inspector, if you had a pharmaceutical problem I would be delighted to try to help, but I was never into Sherlock Holmes."

"Oh well," replied Dobson, "I just wanted to talk to someone about it. To be quite honest, Brock stitched me up so much over his assault on Tanya that I found it hard to have any sympathy. I suspected he had a crooked solicitor, who lied for him, and also think that he bought the magistrate off?"

John looked quickly at Tim and replied, "We didn't know that, but we knew that Tanya never struck him." John was being a little economical with the truth here of course.

The inspector then picked up his bunch of flowers, they then exited the car, said goodbye, and Dobson set off once more for the hospital entrance.

"What did you make of that then?" said Tim clearly a little perturbed.

"Nothing, nothing at all, he is fishing. Top marks to him for coming up with those points, but let's face it; it wasn't rocket science was it?"

"No I don't expect it was really," replied Tim. "Still it was a little unnerving."

"Tim, we have nothing to fear believe me, there is no evidence to link Brock's death with us."

"No but we did have a very good motive," said Tim quietly.

"By the way Tim, you remember me telling you that Lorna was trying to open an outdoor pursuit centre?" Tim nodded. "I know you have mentioned you would like to get out of that place you work at now, and into an outside job; would you like me to tell her you would be interested? You have had quite a lot of experience, with your climbing, pot-holing etc. It could be just what you are looking for."

"Well you could do, but I doubt it would pay enough, I hope to get married soon you know."

It was six months later, Tanya was out of hospital and doing okay. She had to give up her job at the school because her memory was still playing tricks, and she couldn't stand for long periods. She could however ride her horse, and indeed spent much time riding round the village, and visiting Lorna to see how things were progressing at the manor. It was on one such visit that Lorna told Tanya that she would like her to work at the new riding school. Tanya of course was delighted, she was a competent rider, and she thought her chances of getting a job now were slim. Lorna said that if Tim would come to see her, maybe he could have a position at the outdoor pursuit centre. Things were beginning to look up. They wouldn't have to worry about buying a house; Tanya had inherited her parents'. If Tim sold his in Moston, she was sure they could manage okay.

The day of the wedding duly arrived and it was a spectacular affair. Many friends came from Moston, as well as Cragside. A large marquee had been erected on the playing field where the reception would be held, and for the social evening later. John accompanied Tanya gently down the aisle, to the sounds of *Hail the Conquering Hero Comes* and Lorna followed on as the matron of honour. Inspector Dobson was looking on from the back of the church, it seemed as if he might have had something in his eye. Later at the reception after the usual speeches; Lorna asked if she could say a few words.

"I haven't given Tanya and Tim their wedding present yet, I wanted to leave it until now. You will all be aware I am sure that Tanya is not well enough to resume her job teaching. Her surgeon assures us however, that she should make a near full recovery in due time which of course is wonderful news. My wedding present to Tanya then, which is also by way of some compensation for what she has been through, is the new riding school, complete with horses. She will be the owner of one third of the manor, and although I will maintain ownership of the sixteen hundred acres of land, Tanya will have full rights of access written into the deeds.

"My present to Tim is not as grand, but I would like Tim to have the outdoor pursuit centre, I am sure he will make a great success of it, and I wouldn't know where to start. He will also own one third of the manor. By the way the moorland will be open to the public most of the time, so no one should be denied access to my countryside for most of the year."

There were gasps of amazement at this news, then thunderous applause.

"I am perfectly happy to use the remaining third of the manor for my new veterinary practice, which as you know is now up and running. I will not be living there; I am having a cottage built just outside the village. I am sure Tim and Tanya will be looking for any staff they require in the village."

Later when things had quietened down a little Tanya was talking to Lorna. John and Tim were also deep in conversation. Inspector Dobson who was an invited guest approached the two men.

"Been waiting for a chance to speak to you two." It was quite obvious the inspector had had a few drinks he also looked very serious.

"Well Tim, taking over the outdoor pursuit centre then, you should be good at that. I understand you have had some good experience at pursuits. And you doctor John, I understand you have been chasing young Lorna, bet you have done okay there, you are good at bloody chases aren't you?"

Dobson then lifted his glass, took a large swig and turned to walk away. After a couple of paces he stopped turned round with a huge grin on his face, winked and said, "Excuse me gentlemen I'm off for another drink."

Inspector Dobson was moved soon afterwards to Northallerton, about forty miles away. John and Tim would not see him for another year – until in fact the wedding of John and Lorna.

Lorna and John were sitting in the meadow looking down on Black Bog bottom. The Bog was about half a mile wide and two hundred yards across. There were some knurled trees and a few bushes sprouting here and there; but no colour and no birdsong.

"What a funny name, how did it come to be called that?"

"No idea," said John. "It's always been called that as far as I know."

"Is it true you sink if you walk on it?"

"Yes at most times of the year, especially if it has been wet, that's why the fence is there and the danger signs. If we have had a long dry period it is possible to get across, but you have to go quick even then; if you slow down or stop you would be in trouble."

"Why don't they do something about it?"

"They did try. Geologists came round to inspect it. Apparently it is a soak away, for the surface water from the hills. Because of the geology of the ground it is no longer draining, and consequently the soil is now like porridge. They say that in about fifty year's time it will be a lake. Nature will have to take its course."

"What's it like now?" said Lorna. "It's been dry for a couple of weeks."

John looked around and picked up a stout stick. "Let's see shall we?" He threw the stick out into the bog; it landed about twenty yards out, bounced a little and stayed on the crust.

"That's not sinking," said Lorna. A second or two later the stick slowly sank out of sight. "I bet when it turns into a lake this place will be heavenly."

"Yes I am sure it will," agreed John.

"Will you wait here for me a few minutes John, I want to get something?"

"Sure but don't be too long."

Lorna was soon back carrying something in a bag; she sat down and took it out. It was a small casket.

"These are Nathan's ashes John, I didn't know what to do with them, shall we throw them in the bog?"

John had a mental picture of Nathan striking Tanya with the tankard, followed by a picture of a fox being torn apart. Without answering he stood up, took the casket and threw it out on to the bog. It landed well out; sat there for a few minutes as if reluctant to go then slowly sank out of sight. John put his arm round Lorna and said, "Rest in peace Nathan." They turned around and walked back through the meadow of wild flowers to the track above.

Addendum

Twenty-five years have passed. All three businesses are doing well. Tanya and Tim have twin teenage daughters who are now running the riding school. Tim is still running his outdoor pursuits centre. Lorna and John have two boys who are at Leeds University medical school. John is now the much-respected senior general practitioner in the dale. Lorna is only working part time, and spends much of her time horse riding over the moors with Tanya.

Black Bog bottom no longer exists, the geologists got it wrong. It took only twenty years for the lake to develop. What was a bog is now a nature reserve with fish, amphibians and birds in abundance. Nathan it seems got to heaven a little earlier than expected. The lake has found its own level at six foot above the level of the bog; it is now kept at that level by a natural outlet that has formed an overflow stream. This stream runs down through the village to the river. Buxted wood in now partly submerged, and lots of water mammals have now found a new place to live on the edge of the wood. Lorna has named the lake "Nathan's lake" if you ever get to Cragside, be sure to visit it – it really is a lovely spot.

Oh yes, what about Inspector Dobson? I hear you ask. Well, he retired from the police five years ago with a distinguished record. He now works for Lorna running the estate security and maintenance. He and his wife live in a flat above the vet's surgery. He can mostly be found out on the moors in his Land Rover. But sometimes he can be found in the meadow overlooking the lake, with a pensive look in his eyes – for all the world as if he was trying to solve some mystery from the past.

I never did find out whether John told Lorna the truth about Nathan: But then why should I be privy to that information? After all, I am only the village bobby.

Room19

It was a long time since the list of words was produced that people were not allowed to say. These were known as the "Strong Words". It was very difficult at first to avoid using these words, and a certain period of grace was given before punishment started. Rooms had been assigned for punishments 1 to 10, and these were in order of severity. The stronger the word, the higher number the room. No one knew what happened in the rooms, but it was known that nobody had ever been in a room twice. The list of words was long, and they were what could be described as emotive words, similar to these: anger, fear, jealousy, terror, dread, desire, want, punish, like, hate.

Words were constantly being added also. At the top of the list was "love". This was the word that if spoken would get the offender a trip to room 10.

The controllers were gradually getting things as they wanted them, and the people really had no option but to conform. The next edict to come out was control of thought. This was in the early stages of development, and the first trial was to be with the Strong Words. The date was set for the trial period and the people were informed that more rooms, 11 to 20, would be used for thought infringements. Trying not to think the Strong Words was proving very difficult, and when the trial period was over, the rooms were being frequently used. Room 19 however had not been used yet. If the people had been able to think, they would have had thoughts of sheer terror and dread about this room. But because they could not think these words ….

Minerla was to be allowed to meet a young man for the first time. The system was not totally cruel. Although the meeting was only for a brief period, and was to be closely monitored, they could be alone. She was good at control of words and thought, she was a bright girl of sixteen, and had had no problems with the controllers. The couple had been together for about ten minutes, when the alarm sounded. There was nothing unusual about hearing the alarm; it was quite a common occurrence, particularly since the introduction of Strong Words for thought. However Minerla knew at once that she had triggered the alarm. It was her first meeting with a young man, and like any young girl in that situation, she had lost concentration and let her mind wonder. Her thoughts of love were only in the primitive sense, there was no contact allowed between the sexes. All reproduction was done in the controlled area, there was no normal birth here.

The controllers immediately picked up the thoughts, and sounded the alarm. She knew the controllers would not come looking for her, and that she had to report to them herself. This was an extra punishment in itself. She also knew that although there was nothing to keep her in the controlled area, they had all been told many times of the dangers and torments awaiting anyone silly enough to contemplate leaving. Not one person had ever tried to leave. Minerla's thoughts were now running wild, the girl was now totally out of control and breaking all the rules of speech and thought. She knew instinctively that her mistake was severe and would certainly mean she was destined for room 19. The controllers were totally unforgiving, and the fear of the agonies that awaited her in that room was now uppermost in her mind. Then in a state of absolute despair and panic she turned away from the controlled area and slowly made her way towards the perimeter.

She approached the perimeter with great apprehension. She had no idea what the threatened torments consisted of, but she knew there was no choice; she had to proceed now. Two questions now came into her mind. Why had the controllers not come looking for her? They surely knew by now she was not reporting to them, as they would have expected, and why did there not seem to be any deterrent to crossing the perimeter? The only conclusion she could draw from this was that the controllers knew that she knew her destination was room 19. She realised that they would know her only option was the perimeter; the fact that they had shown no concern strengthened her beliefs about what waited for her outside. The controllers knew that the terrors outside the perimeter were even more terrifying than anything in the rooms.

Minerla was sick of life anyway, if this is what it consisted of, she would take her chances. Why did they have to have speech control? Why did they now have to have thought control? Why were people just walking round being frightened all the time? Why couldn't she have a private meeting with a boy and think normal thoughts? What were normal thoughts? She knew she would need all her courage and strength to face what was ahead. She had brought extra sustenance patches with her, and carefully placed one on her arm.

The view across the perimeter was frightening for her; everywhere she looked was dark. Inside of course it was light all the time. Was this one of the terrors she had been warned about, eternal darkness. Plucking up all the courage she could muster she stepped across. The first thing she realised was that the ground instead of being hard was now soft and spongy. She had not experienced anything like this before; everywhere one walked inside the perimeter was hard. She walked on very slowly, greatly relieved that she was free from that place, but terrified at walking blindly into the unknown. What had she to lose? Her sustenance patches would only last ... how long would they last? She didn't know what time was. Inside that place, patches were changed at a given signal; it was all done without thinking.

Minerla now knew that whatever was ahead was nothing to fear. She would never go back, and if she survived long enough to use all her sustenance patches, or encountered real danger, she could always use her termination patch. Maybe that would be the only way left for her. After a short time

Minerla realised that it was not totally dark. When she looked up she could see lots of small lights, and as her eyes adjusted she could sense a stronger light although she couldn't see it. She was glad that at least there was some light however faint, things were not too bad so far. She had no sense of time or distance; these had never been explained or required when she was in that place. But she sensed as she progressed that she was getting safer.

Whilst walking, her thoughts drifted back to the place she had left behind. The Strong Words that they were not allowed to speak – and now not even think, were not words that they had been taught by the controllers. That was why they did not want them used. It was true they had been circulating for a long time, but now the controllers wanted them eliminated. She didn't know why.

Now came the horror, the thing that Minerla had been dreading. The tormentor she had been threatened with was now materialised; a squinting, nearly closed eye was now glaring at her from over the back of a small hill. The fear she felt for room 19 was now surpassed, as she looked in terror at this abomination. She didn't know what colours were; she had only existed in a monochrome environment. There was no need for colour in that place. But if she had known about colours she would have realised that a dull red eye was watching her. She immediately tried to move away, but the eye followed her every step. The eye was now beginning to open and she could feel the warmth of the tormentor's breath.

Soon the eye was wide open and she realised the tormentor was rising upwards as if it was preparing to strike. She had never seen anything like this in her life. She realised she had been a fool to let her mind wonder, instead of staying alert. How could she deal with this evil? Minerla was paralysed with fear.

She didn't know anything about heaven; it just didn't exist in her mind. But if the tormentor had not been there when she had her final look around, she surely must have thought that this was somewhere like heaven. And though she didn't know anything about colours, she could still perceive them, and they fascinated her. When she was eventually able to move again, Minerla, still trembling, took the termination patch from her pouch and carefully removed the protective cover.

She was of course not aware of what she was seeing; but her eyes now scanned a deep blue sky; then dropped to hills and fields which were a beautiful lush green, with splashes of other colours peeping through. She was so sad that she was not going to be allowed to explore and enjoy this place, but how many other abominations were waiting for her? She had seen too much suffering and could not face anymore. She knew that she was being lulled into a false sense of security – she was not about to fall for that.

She had never experienced sleep; people in that place were not allowed to sleep – it just wasn't necessary. Of course because she had never slept, she knew nothing of dreams either. But now the young lady was starting to feel the sensation of fatigue slowly overwhelm her as the patch started to work. She noticed at the same time that although her tormentor was still watching her it did not now seem to be posing so much of a threat.

Minerla then lay down and stretched out on the soft, sweet smelling grass. The slowly rising sun, still watching, gently warmed her sleeping body.

The Transporter

"It is hard to imagine why you commit these offences, what is it that is wrong with you? Surely you have everything you could possibly want, your every wish and desire is catered for. I just cannot understand you at all. You have had numerous chances, and yet you still keep offending. You leave me no alternative this time you will serve ninety years, take him away."

"I object my Lord, I know my client has committed an unforgivable string of offences, but ninety years, how can anybody survive that?"

"He should have thought about that, he has been warned and given every chance to reform, maybe when he gets back he will see the error of his ways."

"But ninety years my Lord, I plead for mercy."

"No mercy, take him away. Next case!"

"My Lord, I appear for the defendant, the charge as you know is not showing you due respect. He does plead guilty, and promises to try to give you the respect you deserve in future."

"How many times has he previously been charged with this lack of respect?"

"Eight times my Lord."

"Has he been warned of the dire consequence on each occasion?"

"He has, my Lord."

"Have you anything to say before I pass sentence."

"Yes my Lord I am truly sorry, I just get carried away and forget that you are responsible for everything. I will try to give you due respect from now on."

"You should have thought of that before, you will serve six years."

"Please my Lord not at that place, I will do anything, I will be better in future, please sir not six years at that place."

"Six years, take him away."

There was much sorrow and crying, as those sentenced were led to the biogenetic transporter. The prisoners had been sentenced to various terms, from one year for very minor offences, to ninety years for the most serious offences. Some were relatively happy at the mercy shown and short sentence given. Others were in complete despair. They knew there was nothing to be done, no way back. When the sentence was passed, it had to be served in full, there was to be no remission.

The biggest punishment was that when they arrived to serve their respective sentences, none of them would have any recollections of why they were there, or indeed were they had come from. They would in effect serve their sentence, in a pre-determined location and situation, and any sentence over ten years would be carefully monitored. Their individual behaviour would determine their level of re-entry.

They had plenty of time to worry about their respective futures on the way to the bio-genetic transporter unit. When the offenders arrived at the transporter, they were individually connected to their pre-programmed locations, and then the bio-genetic technician activated the machine. Only two words flashed up on the red plasma screen to show that the transporter had activated correctly: Earth Bound.

My Pappy Was Always Right

I can never understand why they do it. Most of them are only young, still wet behind the ears, just because they are fast I suppose. The need to be famous? Too much of a risk if you ask me.

Not far to go now. I was heading for Tumbleweed, I had a little business there. Wasn't in any particular hurry, had plenty of time to think about things. Last place I was in, this young guy thought he could take anybody. Yes he was fast, no doubt about that – but not fast enough! Another young guy is bragging he's the fastest now. I wonder how long he will last before someone comes looking for him with something to prove. The madness of these young hotheads.

The sign says "Tumble …", nothing more, (part of the sign is unreadable – shot to pieces) I think it must be the right place though. My pappy was into guns, he made them, told me all about them; now he was fast. I remember pappy telling me that handguns are only accurate fired from the waist over about five yards, after that you need to aim. He told me a rifle was only accurate for fifty yards, after that it was just luck. I worked on his theory and found he was right.

The main thing with any gun is the sights, and I worked a long time getting this right. Speed is necessary, but you have to know that you will hit the target. I practised for hours most days, drawing aiming and firing. I got pretty good. I did the same with rifles; the sights had to be spot on though, they had to be carefully tuned no room for error. This is where a lot of these so-called gunfighters come to grief; they are fast – but tend to ignore their sights. I could hit an apple with my rifle at fifty yards, and a man-sized target at 150 yards. Now that is good shooting. Being fast just isn't good enough, most gunslingers don't use their brain; in many cases their reputation wins them the fight. I worked on a fast draw and then a fast aim. I could get my gun up to my eye, always in the right place, in a split second; this took a great deal of practice, co-ordination was the key. I never worried about anybody's reputation with a gun.

My pappy was into this new scientific thing too. He told me that a bullet fired from a gun level with the ground would hit the ground at the same time as a bullet that is just dropped from the same spot. He said it was to do with the laws of gravity and velocity. Now I didn't know about them laws, I was into a different kind of law – but I believed him. Pappy was always right. After he died, I got a job with the new railroad. I was one of the few who volunteered to go after the fools who thought the railroads had been created for them to rob.

So far I had done okay.

The guy I was coming to see was named Johnny Proctor. We knew he had been involved in a number of attacks on the railroad, and I had been hired to bring him in. I had done some homework and knew a bit about Johnny; yes he was fast, and bragged a lot, never tried to change his appearance or identity. Cocksure he was – no second chances with guys like this. As I approached the small town I knew I was in the right place, the sign over the sheriff's office said Tumbleweed. No one had bothered to shoot this sign up. The sheriff was expecting me. The telegraph message had been received three days before. Johnny Proctor was still in town with his cronies. The sheriff seemed okay, but he made it quite clear to me that his job was to look after the town and stay alive. He was not paid, he told me, to do the railroad's job for them. I understood this okay. He did promise though that he would make sure that things were done in a fair way.

It is always easy to tell the ones who are trouble. There is plenty of work now the towns are growing. There is farm work, cattle and sheep work, there is hotel work, shop work. gunsmiths, blacksmiths, banking, entertainment, no real reason for anyone to be out of work at all The troublemakers didn't want that kind of work though, they needed more money; They were the ones who were always in the saloons, usually drunk, always with the dollar in their pockets, and everyone knew where that dollar came from.

I booked into the best looking hotel in Tumbleweed, had a bath and meal, and then went for a look around the town. I was not wearing my gun, and nobody seemed to take any notice of me. I passed the saloon and heard the usual noise. Yes this place was typical of all the others. I turned in early, needing a good night's sleep. This was hard because of the noise from the saloon, but I eventually dropped off.

I had a good breakfast, tidied up, checked my gun and waited for the noise to start. I didn't have too long to wait. I stopped at the sheriff's to let him know my intention and set off for the saloon. Johnny Proctor was already there with his gang; they had just set their first drinks up and were dealing the cards. Their last job must have been pretty rewarding. I walked up to the bar, ordered a drink and turned to face Johnny.

"Johnny Proctor?" He looked up.

"You talkin ter me stranger?"

"Yep."

"Well it better be good, yer spoiling my game."

"It is good Johnny. I'm here to tek yer in. A little matter of railroad robbery." Johnny put his cards down and slowly stood up.

"I hope yer fast stranger, ain't no one bin fast enough yet."

There was no way I could take him anywhere without a fight, I knew that.

"Well let's go outside Johnny, no point in shooting the saloon up."

Johnny's gang were laughing and not worried, that is until they got outside and saw the sheriff with three deputies each with a shotgun. They knew to keep out of it then. Johnny was cocksure, he didn't seem to have any concern about the distance between us. I was backing away; I needed at least seven or eight yards for safety.

"Getting yellow?" he snarled. "Why don't you just turn round and run?"

I had the distance now and the advantage. Johnny had no idea about my manoeuvre and was sure his speed would determine the outcome. His hand went down, yes he was fast, I drew my gun and turned sideways at the same time that I was sighting Johnny. His gun fired just before mine, he missed – I shot him through the heart.

The sheriff arranged all the details, sent a cable off to my bosses explaining that Johnny wouldn't co-operate and had died in the ensuing shoot out. I knew my pay would be waiting, and next morning I said my goodbyes and set off for home.

About two miles out of town I spotted this guy by the side of his horse.

"Morning to you."

"It ain't a good morning fer you my friend," the stranger answered.

"Oh, and why is that?"

"You're the guy who took Johnny Proctor out. I've bin waiting fer that chance fer months, just arrived in Tumbleweed too late. Still guess it don't matter now. You must be pretty fast? They tell Proctor was handy."

I quickly dismounted, keeping the horse between us. Pappy told me to always do this, and never to shoot from a horse. He said the damn things just won't stay still. Pappy always gave good advice.

"How old are you son?"

"Old enough."

"Old enough fer what?"

"Old enough ter tek you."

"What's yer name son?"

"It's Billy and that's all yer gitten."

"Okay Billy, listen to me …." This young fool was no more than eighteen and I didn't want his blood on my hands,

"Yer see that tree over there?" the tree was about five yards away.

"Yer, I see it"

"Well when I say fire, yer draw and aim fer the tree. I will draw at the same time. The one who hits the tree first is the fastest."

"Okay." Billy turned to the tree, but never took his eyes from me. We were both facing the tree but looking at one another when I said "fire". Billy's gun was out like lightning, I have never seen such a draw; the bark was flying from the trunk before I squeezed my trigger.

"Well I am impressed Billy, yer sure is the greatest. You git back into town now and tell you just outdrew the guy who killed Johnny Proctor, yer the best now son."

"Yep I'll git back ter town now, but I will have you laid across yer saddle, that's the proof I will need."

Billy was no more two yards away when he again drew his gun. This time my gun shot first – Billy dropped dead. Pappy always told me – "Never show anyone how fast you are son, always keep a bit back, git you out of lots of trouble." My Pappy was always right.

I slapped Billy's horse and it galloped off.

I then buried the kid and put a little cross over him. I took my knife out and whittled on the wood: *Here be Billy – just not fast enough.*

It will take me about five days to get back, not in any hurry. Give my beard chance to grow. I will get some new clothes and a new hat; no one will know me.

See you about sometime – maybe.

The Clock

It isn't a very big room; the only thing in it apart from a small table and a chair is a clock on the wall. The clock says one minute past three. I have until four o'clock. My instructions are to write everything down that comes into my mind during this hour. I take that to mean that after four I won't be able to write. I have to tell you (should anyone get to read this) that I have no idea what will happen at four. There is no way of looking out of the room, but I wouldn't want to look out anyway. I have seen enough of out there. I have just had a quick look round to see if there is anything alive in here, I couldn't see anything. It would have been nice to find a spider or fly or something, anything for company.

I wonder how the clock works? Funny thing time, I wonder how timekeeping started? One of those things I always intended to look up but never did. I suppose it started with daybreak, then sun down, that's two divisions. Then sun overhead, mid-day. That's three. Well I suppose after that it was easy to fill in. What was I saying? Oh yes the clock. It looks fairly normal, interestingly though it's analogue, not many of that type still about. Minute hand, hour hand, second hand, temperature gauge. I don't think it is mechanical, no winding point or pendulum thingies. I am tempted to have a closer look.

I used to have a proper mechanical watch, stainless steel it was, Omega Constellation Automatic, dead accurate, never had to wind it. That was a proper watch. I had to give that in long since though, they needed all the metal. What did we get in return? These awful plastic things, well okay – they were accurate, but no personality or character. Tell time anywhere in the world, temperature of wearer, blood pressure, pulse rate, and even weight. All info back into the main frame for continuous monitoring. Did it work? Probably. Did it do any good? No not one bit. What was I saying again? Oh yes, have a closer look at the clock, can't though, been warned not to touch it. Bet it's not battery driven, where would they get the batteries?

Three fifteen now, it's difficult to write like this without any preparation, but I have to keep going. Anybody who reads this will know what has gone on – maybe no one will read it, doesn't matter anyway. I think I have just been told to write to take my mind of the clock. You are probably wondering if I am frightened. No I am not. I have got past that; I just don't care anymore. Why did they pick me though? Okay I am a scientist of sorts, and I was one of those who tried to tell them, would they listen? Of course not, did they ever? We all know now that they were just doing what all the rest have done – look after themselves. The fools; well they are in the same mess now, I suppose that is one consolation, for all the good that will do.

WW1 was the war to end all wars, that was until WW2 came along. Did they learn anything? No, not a thing. United States of Europe – what a joke. Still it's too late now. Three thirty, only half an hour. Expect I can keep writing something. We told them that underground nuclear power stations were needed and plenty of them. We told them fossil fuels were running out. What did they do? Left it too late. Well that's true to form. We told them about unchecked immigration, about lack of water, about pollution. The consequences were so predictable to all but those who could have stopped it. Well it's too late now.

I had everything back then. In fact I always said I achieved far more than I deserved. Life was kind to me. It's all gone now – the lot. The only way I stopped going mad was to train myself not to think about it. Three forty: not long to go. I wonder what's going to happen at four? Why didn't they tell me? It's quite exciting really; things can only get better. I hate to think about those poor souls still out there. I wonder if this was meant to happen – I mean, was it pre-ordained? Strange that it happened all over the world at the same time. We really have been so stupid, the trouble has always been that those in power always thought that they were right, and mostly as we now know, they were all wrong.

It seems without doubt that we were the only place in the entire universe that had life. What did we do? We killed the bloody lot, well nearly. Not much left now. I expected it though, the writing was on the wall many years ago and nobody took note. The governments tried to give the people what they wanted – and look where it got us. Don't know what to write now – running out of words; still don't think anybody will read this anyway, Tra la la la la.

Three fifty, I wish I could have one last look out. Still, probably not. Better just try to remember the good things. My goodness, I had more than my share of them. Yes I have been pretty fortunate really, had lots of things, plenty of money, nice house, nice car, nice family – all gone now. Tra la la la la. Am I getting a bit nervous now? No, not possible.

Quite looking forward to four, nothing else to look forward to. Hope you can get to read this rubbish, been a long time since I wrote with a pen. I am going to keep writing right up till four, it will keep my mind of things, tra la la la la. Just trying to remember the good times now. If only those idiots had listened, things could have been so different. Well it's nearly time, just a couple of minutes; longest hour I have ever experienced.

Three fifty-nine, I wonder what is powering the clock? Not a bad looking clock really I have seen worse – tra la la la la, It's three fifty-nine fifty-five now, last cou ...

It isn't a very big room; the only thing in it apart from a small table and a chair is a clock on the wall. The clock says one minute past three. I have until four o'clock.

My instructions are to write everything down that come into my mind during this hour. I take that to mean that after four I won't be able to write. I have to tell you (should anyone get to read this) that I have no idea what will happen at four.

*

Tom Brewer is what you would call a know-it-all, he is also known as Mr Pontificator, but not to his face. I suppose we all know at least one; he knows everything about everything, and is never wrong. The vicar on the other hand, is a hard working guy, pandering to his church duties and flock by day, and unwinding a little at night. Harry Oats is known as Mr Pipe – but not to his face either; he never says much at all, he always has his flat cap on and his pipe in his mouth. One can tell if he is in tune with conversation by the way his pipe traverses his bottom teeth; if he is interested in anything his pipe reciprocates faster. Maisie Simmons is the odd one out, about thirty-five and very attractive. She arrived at this Yorkshire village a few days after the reported sighting on the moor. She apparently represents a government department. So there you have our quartet. They have formed a strange group, who of late meet every evening for a drink or two, in the local hostelry.

On this particular evening Tom had just finished explaining to the vicar how to run his church, in between drinking his Lager. The vicar was sipping his medium white wine and smiling kindly. Mr Pipe was obviously not overly impressed at the conversation, his pipe hardly moving; only removed from his mouth enough for him to take sips of his Barley Wine. Miss Maisie was drinking a sherry and occasionally interrupting Tom to correct any particularly inaccurate statements.

Mr Pontificator was stopped in full flow when the pub door opened and in walked the stranger. He was a tall well-built man with a confident manner. He stopped after a couple of paces into the pub, looked around at the eyes that were perusing him, and at the now silent mouths; he bowed in greeting, and proceeded to the bar. The talking now continued and eyes returned to their original places. (This is the normal procedure for any stranger entering a Yorkshire hostelry). He was greeted courteously by the landlord, and offered a room for the night. In answer to his question about food, he was offered ham and eggs, tomatoes, mushrooms and chips. The stranger then went to his room to change and shower, he would be down for the meal in twenty minutes.

The landlord was just bringing the food to the dining room table as the stranger came down. He now looked more casual, and took his seat with just the merest glances from the regulars. The stranger ate his meal with relish, and washed it down with hot tea. After a few minutes he stood up and walked to the bar, and asked for a pint of best. He was presented with a pint of Old Peculiar, took a sip, smiled, then turned and glanced around him. The vicar caught his eye, stood up and asked the stranger if he would like to join them. The stranger nodded and walked over to their table.

"This is Maisie Simmons – Tom Brewer, Harry Oats, and I am the local vicar." The stranger shook their hands in turn and then introduced himself.

"I am Pythagoras Rosso."

Harry Oats' pipe was now slowly traversing his bottom teeth. The vicar remarked, "What a magnificent name." Miss Maisie gave a slight smile, and Mr Pontificator launched straight in.

"Ah Pythagoras, I know about him. It was him that got a bath one night, noticed the water spilling over the side, and worked out a formula."

Maisie was quick to reply, "I think you have the wrong man Tom, that was Archimedes."

"I have always been interested in Pythagoras, Mr Rosso. Was it not he who taught about the transmigration of the soul? And if I remember correctly his philosophy influenced Plato to some degree."

"You are correct Miss Simmons, but I do believe he had a flair with numbers also," answered Mr Rosso with a wink.

Maisie smiled at Pythagoras, and Tom said, "Well yes I knew all that", before taking a long drink, realising he was way out of his depth.

Mr Rosso appeared to be greatly impressed by Maisie's knowledge, and obviously realised that she was a very educated young woman.

She was in fact in Yorkshire investigating a reported sighting of a meteor impact. The vicar was one of the people who claimed to have seen the impact; he was a keen stargazer. The Yorkshire moors are known to be one of the best spots for watching the heavens on a dark evening, there being no distracting ground light. The site of the impact, which the vicar and a few others had claimed to see, had not yet been discovered. Maisie had some scientific instruments with her, and as well as being out alone, she had spent some time on the moors with the vicar.

The vicar was adamant that there had been an impact, but there was still a vast area to cover. He then asked Pythagoras if he would care to join him on the moors the next day, it being the vicar's day off. He said he would be delighted to, and then asked to be excused because he was tired and wanted an early night. Shortly afterwards Maisie went to the ladies room, followed soon after by Mr Pipe who went to the Gents. A few minutes later Mr Pipe returned to his seat, clearly agitated; the pipe was now traversing at a great speed across his bottom set.

"What on earth's the matter with you Harry?" exclaimed Tom.

"Well when I came out of the Gents and passed the stairs to the bedrooms, I could hear Maisie talking to that Pythag bloke up at the top."

"It wouldn't have been Maisie," said the vicar. "Why would she go upstairs to talk to him? It must have been the landlord's wife checking he was okay."

Just then Maisie returned, sat down and finished her sherry. She then asked the vicar if maybe she could join them on the moors the next day. This was agreed, and she then asked to be excused as she had some work to do. Harry was clearly still affected by something, his pipe still moving rapidly.

"Sumatt funny going on here," he muttered, without removing his pipe from his mouth. "I am sure it was Maisie talking up the stairs."

He would have thought there was something funny going on if he could have seen through the ceiling above his head. Maisie was just removing her last garment before climbing into bed with Pythagoras ....

Mendip Hill is a Royal Air Force establishment by name. It is however the home for one of the world's largest communication and signal tracking stations. The base is actually run by American civilians, and service personnel. It is at Clayhouses in North Yorkshire, England. It is also very near to the moors and the village. It is claimed that Mendip Hill can access any radio signal, analogue or digital. It can apparently access any computer traffic. It can also, it is thought – with the help of British intelligence – decipher any coded messages.

I must add here that people have been protesting at this base for years, the protesters want it closed down. They now fear it is part of the "Star Wars" programme. It was to be expected then that Mendip Hill was certainly aware of the alleged meteor landing. They not only knew about that, having tracked it in, but were also aware of radio signals from the area which they so far had not been able to decode. Mendip Hill was certainly not asleep.

Pythagoras, Maisie, and the vicar met outside the church as arranged the next morning, checked their equipment (one doesn't venture on to the moors, even for just a day without certain precautions). All was in order and the three set off. Pythagoras was keen to know where the vicar placed the location of the apparent impact. It seemed that his sighting was about three in the morning. The vicar had found out about the expected shooting star display from his internet contacts; he had also read about it in the papers. It had been eagerly anticipated. The best views would be on the moors, as high as possible, between two and four in the morning. The vicar explained that it had been a superb display, and said about half way through there seemed to be an impact. He had been back to the area alone and with Maisie a number of times looking, but admitted he could be miles out with his estimation.

Maisie then shocked the vicar. "No vicar, you are not miles out, in fact you are very near. I have been waiting for clearance to tell you." Pythagoras then nodded at Maisie and she continued. "What you saw was not a meteorite or meteor; we picked that time of activity for our arrival, hoping we would not be observed."

Pythagoras then interjected, "What you actually saw was the arrival of a time machine."

The vicar stood open-mouthed fully expecting the duo to burst into laughter, however they remained deadly serious.

Maisie continued, "We had to make contact in 2006-2008 if we were to stand any chance of altering the impending disaster. We are from the not too distant future, and all our technology for the last one hundred and fifty years has gone into this machine. We may have got it operational just in time. We had to choose our landing site with great care, obviously to arrive without any collisions with buildings and to arrive if possible unobserved. The moors were ideal, the timing was perfect; but alas even then we were spotted. However I can tell you that you would never have found our machine."

Pythagoras added, "We have been quite lucky in finding you vicar, we have much to talk with you about. First though we will show you our machine since we are so near to it."

The vicar was clearly shaken by what he had just heard, and was having difficulty taking it in, as you can imagine. It was whilst they were approaching the top of an incline that the military men appeared. The officer in charge approached the three and looked straight at Maisie.

"Maisie Simmons," he said in a cold voice,

"Yes that's me," said Maisie looking a bit worried.

"We have been watching you and checking, we have some questions to ask you. You claim to work for a Government agency, however our checks reveal no one of your name or description is working for any Government agency. There is also the matter of unexplained radio transmissions. Please come with us. We will want to speak to you two gentlemen also, you can return to the village now but don't leave – you will be watched."

"Damn and Blast," said Pythagoras as Maisie was led away. "I knew this time thing would get us into trouble, but I didn't expect it so soon."

"Doesn't Maisie work for the government then?" said the vicar.

"Yes, she certainly does vicar, but not in 2006, actually in the year 2155 – our first mistake I fear."

Pythagoras caught up with the military group, and told them that Maisie and he were together, in fact that they were man and wife. He explained that what they had to reveal would be best done together, and if possible with their friend the vicar present. There was no objection to this, and the party left the moor together. Maisie now found that the people they were to talk with were government intelligence officers, and some officials from Mendip Hill. They were driven to Clayhouses in a military vehicle, and into the base. They were then led into a large room and directed to seats.

Before anyone had time to speak, Maisie stood up and said, "You will find what we are about to tell you will be very difficult to believe, however before you question us and ridicule our story we must tell you that we are able to prove what we say. My husband and I are from the future, actually the year 2155. We will give you full computerised detail later, but now we will give you a brief statement of why we are here."

Pythagoras continued, "The world is heading for disaster, this present time is the only time that can influence the outcome. We are here to try to change the future. Let me tell you the state of the world in 2155. We have to be careful not to moralise; so will stick just to facts.

"The world we have left is a total disaster area. It is full of sick and dying people. The lands will no longer produce crops because of chemicals. The seas are all now lifeless because of over-fishing and pollution. There are no functioning police or medical services, no hospitals. There are no fossil fuels left, and no ships sail the seas anymore. With respect to the UK – the channel tunnel and the bridges we had built across to France had to be blown up some time ago. This was to stop the spread of disease brought in from Asia and Africa. Our once powerful antibiotic drugs are now completely useless. Unchecked immigration has swamped our island.

"It is thought that all life is finished in Asia. Africa was completely wiped out by disease, apart from a small section of the north. The last we heard from America was total disaster, if there is life at all it is in isolated pockets. Europe is devastated – Britain seems to be the last functioning place, but not for long. Communication is virtually impossible, television and radio is a thing of the past. The loss of satellite function has stopped all telephone traffic. People are expecting the state to provide for them, and are mostly unable to do what little work there is. Unfortunately the government such as it is, has no resources left. There are no means to maintain the elderly. People do not reach sixty, and many die much younger. We have come from an infertile dying world of disease, misery, and despair."

"The reasons for this disaster?" Maisie prompted.

"Well look no further than these possibilities, not necessarily in any order. Religious fanaticism, abuse of drugs, sexually transmitted diseases, and unrestricted immigration. We have also had a complete breakdown in law and order and have hardly any fuel supplies left. What I have mentioned here are the points which we think were the catalyst for the troubles, you could add more as you will see. In this box you will find a full graphical computerised chronology from now until 2155. Do not worry about compatibility we have made sure your toy computers will be able to handle it." Pythagoras managed a smile at this point. The vicar and others present were staring opened mouth as the couple related their message.

"How have you survived, and even managed to build a so called time machine under those circumstances?" was a not unexpected question from one of the officers.

Pythagoras replied, "We are a group of professionals and intellectuals who anticipated the coming problems some time ago. We are under constant threat and are repeatedly invaded for our supplies. However because we have never taken drugs and are all reasonably intelligent, we have been easily able to outwit our attackers. We have good defences, but our time is now rapidly running out. Maybe it was your grandchildren who had the foresight to jump ship so to speak. They set up a community, which is not far from here, and made it self sufficient and supporting.

"Among us are Engineers, Doctors, Scientists and Physicists. We exist mainly now on synthetic food, our original stockpiles are just about done. There are of course no animals to eat; they are all long gone. In fact our scientists and engineers only just managed to finish this machine in time, we estimate six months is all we have left to live. Fortunately one of the guys who joined our group about fifty years ago had been working on this project for some time. Most of the hard work had been done; the machine had been under development for many years according to our facts. We were indeed fortunate to acquire the details. We have to tell you also that we only had enough propellant to get here, unless you can supply us with our needs we can never return and the Earth will be doomed."

Pythagoras handed over a long formula to the group, and the details were immediately typed into a computer. He looked relieved when the computer confirmed the compound could be made. It seemed they could at least return, if they were allowed to.

"So what you are saying," said the man who appeared to be in charge, "is that if we don't change the way we are running the world, we only have just over hundred and fifty years to go?"

"That's it in a nutshell," said Maisie.

Pythagoras, Maisie and the vicar were led into an adjoining room, and left alone with a guard. A short time later a gentleman they hadn't seen before joined them.

"I am interested in your story of a time machine. We have actually just started working on such a project. From what you say it will take 150 years to develop."

"Well that would seem to be the case," said Pythagoras. "But we have been many years just testing since its completion. It has been here on trial runs, but apart from very early tests, this is the first time it has carried anyone. It was a tremendous risk, but we had nothing to lose. I was in fact the first person to test it in an early version. I was only able to go back in time just one hour in that original test." The group were called back into the room. The officer who seemed to be in charge then said with raised eyebrows, "Obviously we will have to see your machine – it is only because we are aware that work has started on such a machine that we are prepared to listen to you. We will inspect your machine tomorrow. You will all have to stay here tonight. Vicar, you may use the phone to give some excuse for your absence."

The next morning found the group driving towards the moors. The vehicles were soon abandoned and the party set off on foot. Some time later Maisie stopped and exclaimed, "Okay this is it." The vicar was the first to declare that he could not see anything.

"Well we told you that you would never find our machine vicar," replied Maisie. "The simple reason why is because it is not here. Obviously we could not risk it being found so we programmed it to go forward a short way; we will now bring it back."

Pythagoras took an instrument from his pack, made some adjustments and pressed a button.

"We had enough power for this short trip forward and backwards, it should be appearing any second now." Slowly a small circular capsule took shape in front of them.

"We had to stay apart for some time after our arrival," said Maisie. "That would explain the radio signals. We used very low power laser radios to communicate; you did well to pick up the signals. You would never have decoded them though." Nobody in the party seemed to hear what Maisie had said; they were all staring in amazement at the machine.

"You will understand that it is not possible for you to inspect our time machine gentlemen," said Pythagoras. We can not give any physical help to you, but we have left a clue to a major problem you will encounter. This you will find that on the computer programme we left you."

"Is it possible to go into the future?" This question came from the vicar.

"No," said Maisie, "that will never be possible, one cannot go into what has not occurred. However if Pythagoras and I stayed away for a year, when we returned to our time, we would be able to go forward another year. In that respect we would be going into our future by one year. But of course that year would have already passed. We would in effect just be catching up. I hope you can understand that." The nod of heads seemed to indicate that the explanation had been understood.

"Now we will load our fuel rods and prepare to return to our time. If we return here, we will be back at this same spot in exactly ten minutes. If however we find things just the same as when we left, we have decided we will stay in our time and die with our friends." All those present knew there was nothing to be done but to agree.

As the two travellers were preparing to leave, the vicar stepped forward. "God bless you both, and thank you for your efforts to help us and future generations. Just one last question. Does anyone believe in God in 2155?"

Maisie embraced the vicar, kissing him tenderly on his cheek and said, "Yes vicar they do. We have a small church in our community." The vicar kissed Maisie back, then shook Pythagoras warmly by the hand. The ministry men came forward and shook hands, and the military men saluted. A few seconds later the capsule quietly disappeared. Two hours later the vicar and the officials decided there was no point in waiting any longer. They silently left the moor.

The story of course eventually made the press. Television and radio had been discussing nothing else for the last month. World leaders were busy discussing the computer programmes, and serious efforts were being put in place to stem what was perceived to be a downward spiral to destruction. Academics were saying they were wasting their time. Because the capsule didn't return, obviously things were not going to alter. Everyone would have to accept it; the warnings had been there for some time; but had been ignored. Nothing could be done.

In the pub the vicar now only had two companions. Mr Pontificator had been very quiet of late. Mr Pipe had had very little pipe movement, and the vicar was trying to put a brave face on things. He had been having much trouble with his congregation though. Mr Pipe had just taken a sip of his barley wine when his pipe started to move – almost imperceptibly at first, but definite movement. It gradually increased speed until it was reciprocating as fast as anyone had seen it go. Both the vicar and Tom were staring at Harry now.

"What on earth is bothering you Harry?" said the vicar and Tom both together.

"I have been thinking about what you told us about the time machine thing," said Mr Pipe. Maisie and Pythagoras told you they would not return if things were the same when they got back to 2155."

"Yes that's correct," said the vicar.

"But what if things were normal?" said Mr Pipe. "What if there was no sickness, no hunger, no wars, no major problems at all."

"I don't follow," said the vicar.

"Well," said Mr Pipe, "history for them would have been totally different. What I am saying is, they most probably would not have known anything about their trip here, nobody would. It would not have been necessary. There may not even have been a time machine; there may not have been a reason to build one. They maybe couldn't have made the return trip. It seems to me, that Pythagoras and Maisie did what they set out to do, they did alter the future. They are probably both living a normal life now, or will be in their time 2155."

Harry Oats had removed his pipe and cap placed them on the table and was now smiling – The vicar slowly stood up patted Harry on the shoulder, and then shouted out something you would never expect a Yorkshireman to say: "The drinks are on me."

The Indian Rope Trick

Most people if they are honest, will have had some personal experience, or at least will have heard of some story or occurrence that seems to defy logic. At best it may be difficult to believe, or it may well be impossible to believe. The problem arises of course when the occurrence that is being related to you comes from a person of high intellect and standing, and who happens to be a personal friend.

Humphry is the vicar of our rural church, and Ken is an active member of the church committee. We are all good friends and try to meet at least every two weeks if possible, for a meal and a couple of drinks. We have got into the habit of late to take it in turns to relate any occurrences that we have experienced in our lives that would be interesting to the others. I had been told some quite extraordinary stories by my two friends, which had always been interesting and entertaining. And I would like to think that when it has been my own turn they would have found my stories similarly entertaining and perhaps a little thought provoking. However nothing could have prepared us for the tale we were about to hear. Humphry's related experience really stunned us. We both wanted to know why he had left it so long to tell us about this event in his life, which would obviously create much interest. His answer was very predictable. He was not the kind of guy who would knowingly try to go one better, or upstage anyone, and although he was obviously greatly impressed by the events he described to us, he was also quite disturbed. He was a man who liked to be able to explain things, as indeed are most of us, however in this case he was totally puzzled.

You will now be beginning to realise why he shared this story, he wanted Ken and I to try to evaluate it with him and maybe come up with some plausible explanation. He agreed that I could write this account of his experience, and I will write it as if Humphry is telling the story himself. He will of course read it before you do, so you can be sure it is entirely accurate. I would ask you to try to refrain from judgment until you have read the whole story. This is the story that Humphry told to Ken and I:

"Many years ago when I was at college studying for my Theology degree, we arrived at the point when all students in my year were required to venture out into the outside world, to do some external work towards their final thesis. The choice was really left up to the individual but there was support and guidance available to those who were unsure about what to do. This could of course have been through financial restraint or purely just not knowing what to look for.

Many went to schools to practice teaching, others who were probably hoping to go into the ministry chose to be attached to a church. I fully intended to go into church ministry, but wanted to study other religions at first hand. Fortunately in my case, coming from a family that didn't have any problems financially, and having already decided where I wanted to go, I had no such concerns. I would go to India.

"The subcontinent of India had always fascinated me. I, like many others I suppose, had read much about the country, but to my regret, I had not had the opportunity to go until now. My main desire to go there was to study the many diverse and different religions, and although I knew that time would be short, it would be a great chance for me to extend my knowledge of eastern religions.

"It was then, to my great delight that over dinner that evening, the two people I had developed a close friendship with, expressed a desire to go to India. David Mason was a quite brilliant student who went on to obtain a double doctorate. Lorna Crest, a similarly brilliant young lady, went on to become a research biologist. These two young people had a deep interest in theology hence their studying for a degree in the subject, however neither of them had any intention of pursuing it as a profession. I have to say that they seemed to be thinking that a trip to India would be something of a holiday for them.

"The next obstacle was to convince the Dean that our trip was feasible and that it would be productive. The Dean was no stranger to my family; we had been friends for many years. I knew that he would have no objections to my going, he well knew of my desire to study other religions, and knew also that I had no financial worries. I was concerned however for David and Lorna, they were not in the same fiscal situation as myself, and the Dean was well aware of this fact.

"I decided a prudent word with my father before their meeting would be in order. My father decided that if I was to be let loose on the Indian subcontinent I would need at least two mature and stable companions to accompany me, and he was willing to sponsor the whole cost if they indeed were suitable. The Dean was already in possession of this knowledge before my two friends had their interviews. The Dean had no objections. At this stage of the proceedings neither of my friends knew my father was sponsoring them, they thought that they were getting a grant through the university for further study abroad.

"The timing was just about perfect; we were to go in early January, a very nice time to go to India, well clear of the monsoon and still relatively cool, at least by their standards. At the time we went, we were not of course able to take advantage of frequent schedule not stop flights, or even charter flights, I will not bore you with travel details only to say it took longer than it would today. We thoroughly enjoyed the journey though and arrived safely."

Humphry paused at this point and wanted to tell us a little about the Indian religions. He emphasised that what he would tell us was not definitive, but he told us it would be interesting. He included details of the Buddhist, and Sikh religions, but as they are not really pertinent to this story I have left that part out and just left in the part about the Hindu religion.

He continued, "I had done an in depth study of Islam at college and it was now my intention to divert my attention to the Hindu, religion. Unfortunately we had arrived too late for me to study Diwali, the festival of light that follows the end of the monsoon period, however I was welcomed into the Mandir (Temple) by the priests. I have no intention of boring you with religious theories, that is not the point of this story. However I need to tell you a little. The ancestors of the Hindus settled the Hindu valley as early as 2000 BC, they were a white Aryan race and it is thought they came from Siberia. It was these people who it is thought created the names for the life forces which they worshiped, and indeed many of these Gods are still worshiped by the modern Hindus. This of course explains why some Indians have very pale skins, the indigenous people obviously bred with the incoming Aryans.

"It would not be fair to my two friends to say that they had not expressed, or even attempted to gain any more knowledge of the Indian religions, other than what they knew before our trip. However it would be true to say their interest had been minimal. I personally was not concerned about their activities; I was too involved and fascinated to be bothered. Each evening over dinner we exchanged details of our daily activities, which were very seldom spent together. I have to say that they seemed to be having a great time and thoroughly enjoying their holiday.

"To be perfectly honest by the end of the day I was happy to forget Indian religion, and listen to the accounts of my friend's days out as we enjoyed our evening meal. Both David and Lorna had a great fascination for things mystical, and these were indeed the things they were eager to tell me about each evening. India as you will know is steeped in mysticism, some things can be easily explained as trickery, but some things seem to defy any explanation. It was the latter that my friends were interested in.

"On the beach one morning they had witnessed something that they were unable to understand. An Indian family had appeared near the beach to entertain, as they apparently frequently do, and a crowd had soon gathered, (as they frequently do). Most of the spectators were of course indigenous people there for a free show, which they have probably seen hundreds of times. However there is always a smattering of foreigners happy to be deprived of their rupees.

"The performance had consisted of acrobatics, tightrope walking, and juggling, quite a normal repertoire for these sort of shows it seems. What created the excitement however was the final act. Two young children of about nine or ten, a boy and a girl, had apparently formed themselves into the shape of a wheel. They then rolled down a slope onto the sand, by this time they were travelling quite fast, after a few yards the wheel stopped, and only one of the children was still there. David and Lorna of course soon worked out that the missing child was in a secret location in the sand, over which they had rolled.

This however was not the case, the sand was dug over and examined, the performance was again repeated, and this time the other child disappeared. My friends were completely baffled. I of course could not help; it sounded like an excellent trick to me nothing more.

"The next day I was talking to the Hindu priest who I had made friends with, and I mentioned the trick, which had baffled my friends. He would have been a 'fakir' was his reply. He went on to explain fakirs were Hindu ascetics or holy men, originally a mendicant dervish, he told me there were similar Muslim fakirs, and the word was of Arabic origin meaning poor man. He clearly did not want to discuss the subject anymore, but told me to tread with care, he said fakirs had amazing abilities, and should be shown enormous respect.

"That evening my friends were again very excited. They had apparently witnessed 'The Indian rope trick' and we spent an entire evening trying to work out how it was done. At bedtime we had run out of ideas, it had been an interesting evening. Our time in India had alas run out. We had all thoroughly enjoyed it, although in different ways, but I was sure my friends would have no problem convincing anyone of the value it had been to them. If I had been asked to predict the results of our final examinations I would have put both David and Lorna down for straight firsts. I am not wishing to brag but of course I was spot on, no surprise there; the surprise was that I obtained a 2.1, I was delighted as examinations were never my strong point, I think sheer determination got me through. It speaks volumes for my friends when I tell you that a lot of the examination was devoted to Indian religion. Wherever did they pull the information from?

"It was now time to part company. We were all heading in different directions and pursuing different professions, we made the usual promises that we would keep in touch, and I am pleased to tell you that we did. I won't bore you with the intervening period prior to me obtaining my first Parish as a fully ordained priest. I of course had to pursue the relevant training, take a number of assistant jobs, and do a spell as a hospital chaplain. The parish I was offered was in the centre of a large city and it only had a small congregation, it was a large church and my attitude was that things could only get better.

"During my settling in period at the church, I made it my business to get to know the leaders at the various religious buildings in the area. One of the people I met was the priest at the local Hindu Temple. He was a very quiet and unassuming gentleman, and also very friendly, he had achieved the highest position in his religion of Brahman. He was obviously delighted that I had taken the trouble to look him up, and was pleasantly surprised to find out that I had some knowledge of his religion and that I showed an interest in it. We met quite a few times over the following months, and it was on one of these occasions that I got round to telling him of my trip to India. I also told him quite light heartedly of my two companions and where most of their interest had been.

"He immediately became very interested and asked me if I could remember what had particularly impressed them. The only two things that came to mind were the rolling children on the beach and the rope trick, I had to tell him of course that I had not seen these performances myself, but was able to tell him that my friends were indeed impressed. I also told him of the priest in India who had told us that what my friends had seen would have been performed by a fakir. The priest then told me that this was not necessarily so. He went on to tell me that in the early days of Colonialism, and the East India Company, what is now referred to as 'The Indian Rope Trick' was only referred to as 'The Rope' by Indians. He said further that because the soldiers of this period were not able to accept that what they were seeing couldn't be anything other than a trick, they were the ones who coined the phrase The Indian Rope Trick. Of course the indigenous people of the period were very keen to relieve the soldiers of their rupees, and many clever charlatans appeared on the scene willing to demonstrate The Indian Rope Trick, to the gullible troops; who were well known for drinking too much. My Hindu friend then told me he would tell me how they performed The Indian Rope Trick. This then is what the Brahman told me: '*First you have to understand that people who go to see a performance of this kind, go with the intention of believing what they see. Many people are on record as being willing to give a year of their lives to see the rope trick, and indeed one has to regard oneself as extremely lucky to see a performance, it is not done frequently. Genuine fakirs would not normally perform for money; therefore one must be aware, that if money has been paid, the performance you may have seen, however good, could well have been The Indian Rope Trick, and not The Rope.*

The trick can be done in a number of ways; in the West you are well aware of mass hypnotism, and this is one of the ways. At one performance a photograph was taken of the rope with child ascending, but when developed there was no rope or child only the fakir gesticulating.

Another way is to have a rope made of hundreds of small pieces of jointed bamboo, painted to look like a rope. When the rope is thrown in the air a chord is pulled that runs through it, and the rope then locks enough for a small child to climb up. Usually this trick will be performed under a tree, the boy can then disappear in the foliage and an assistant in the tree then pulls the rope up. Truly a case of what you want to believe.

Now I will tell you what it is like to observe The Rope. The fakir will produce the rope and ask for it to be inspected, he then throws the rope in the air, it straightens and hovers about four feet from the ground. The rope can be twenty to thirty feet long. A young boy or girl then shins up the rope, the fakir then makes the appropriate signs and the climber and rope disappear. This type of performance is never done under a tree, or any other structure. The climber then appears some distance away and walks back to the fakir. This type of performance is only seen once in a lifetime.'

"What can one say to that? The Brahman was obviously being sincere, but how can anybody believe that story? He instinctively knew that I couldn't believe what he had just related, and what he said next was astounding. Before he became a Brahman, my friend told me that he had been a fakir. The best way he could describe modern day fakirs was to relate them to our monks, i.e. not often seen, but nevertheless still about. He had apparently spent many years in total poverty, studying and praying in private. During this time of deprivation he had also studied mysticism as all fakirs do. This is the reason why they are seldom seen in public, and why anyone who sees one perform is indeed lucky.

"What the priest said next was amazing; because of my interest in him and his religion, and because I had showed him true friendship, he was prepared to demonstrate The Rope to me. He had already anticipated the question that I was about to ask, and said that of course if my two friends were able to attend they would be most welcome. I duly contacted David and Lorna, and they were staggered at what I told them. Of course they wanted to come. We had a little trouble finding a suitable time that was convenient for the four of us, but eventually homed onto a couple of days that were suitable, and the date was set.

"There was to be no intrigue about where we would see the performance, it was to be in the Temple, the only sad thing about that, was the fact that it had once been a church. The advantage was that it was high. David and Lorna had arrived late the previous night, tired and hungry. We didn't stay up talking for long, and we all had a good night sleep. In the morning, we arrived at the Temple at the appointed time to find the priest already there. There was a basket in the middle of the temple, and nothing else. I introduced my two companions to the Brahman, they were noticeably excited, and he was noticeably calm!

"He explained the procedure. Once he had started we must not make any sound, we could pick anywhere to observe from, and would have chance for more closure observation later on. He then asked if we had any questions before he started. I think that we probably would all have liked to ask some introductory questions, but I was glad my two colleagues thought it prudent to stay quiet as I did. I took up position just behind and slightly to the right of the Priest; Lorna was facing us, about two yards behind the basket. David was some distance to my right. The Priest then took the cover from the basket, bent over and lifted a heavy gauge rope from the basket. The rope was neatly coiled, and both ends were bound to prevent fraying. Without any ado he then tossed the rope into the air, the end snaked upwards until it was vertical, it stopped just touching the ground, then very slowly started to rise again until it was about three feet from the floor. I snatched a quick glance at Lorna and David at this point; I just couldn't begin to describe the looks on their faces.

"We hadn't heard any sounds at all, but two children now stood behind us, a boy and girl of about nine or ten, both of Eastern origin, and dressed as such. Without any prompting the boy walked up to the rope and started to climb up with effortless ease. When the boy reached the top he paused, looked down briefly, and then disappeared.

"Up to this point I would have had a good idea how things had been done, now I was completely bewildered. The girl stayed where she was, and the priest then called us together. He told us that behind the drapes at the sides of the temple, we would find two A-frame stepladders, which were used, for decorating high points, cleaning, and changing lights etc. If we wanted to inspect the top of the rope we were invited to get the steps and do so; however we were under no circumstances to touch the rope. David placed one ladder at one side of the rope about one yard away, and I did the same at the other side, we then slowly climbed up.

"The top of the rope was about twenty feet high, and as the steps were perfectly stable we were able to reach level with the top of the rope. We both stretched out our arms and could touch hands directly over the rope. There was a good ten feet to the ceiling of the temple, and nothing between the top of the rope and the ceiling but space. David said, 'how on earth did he do that.' I didn't answer and started down the ladder. Just as we reached the floor we noticed that the boy was now stood at the side of the girl again. This time the girl stepped forward and started to climb the rope, as she reached the top the rope fell to the floor and the girl had disappeared. The Brahman then coiled up the rope and put it carefully in the basket. He led the way out of the temple followed by Lorna, David and myself, following behind was the boy, and yes the girl.

"Outside the temple the priest bade us farewell, he knew we would be eager to discuss what we had just observed, and he looked forward to seeing me soon, and hoped he would meet David and Lorna again sometime. We all shook hands with him, and then we gave him and the children the traditional Indian greeting, bowing with hands prayer-like in front. The children beamed at us, then turned and walked away. David was the first to speak, he was sure the children in the temple were the same two who had done the 'wheel' when we were in India. This was clearly ridiculous and wasn't mentioned again, after all most Indian children look alike, don't they?

"The next morning I was showing Lorna and David around my church. I was delighted to hear that they both still attended their respective churches regularly, and the genuine interest that they showed. David jokingly asked me if I was still rich. I told him that a vicar should not be seen to be rich, indeed he should not be rich. Although I had been very privileged in my early days, things were now very different. I explained that I had put enough away to buy a house when I retired, I had enough to provide a small car, although I used a cycle when possible. I told them that I had used a great deal of my own money to do repairs to the church, which was in an awful state of repair when I arrived. David is a decent organist, and with my blessing was soon giving Lorna and myself a recital. When he had finished playing he told us that the organ had some problems. I explained that indeed the organ was the next item on our agenda. We were currently trying to raise about five thousand pounds, which had been quoted for the repair. He promised to leave me a few pounds and wished us well in our efforts.

"The last meal we had together before my friends left was fairly subdued, partly because we would soon be parting again, and partly because none of us could come up with any plausible explanation to what we had witnessed. We had in fact not spoken about it much at all, and had been quite happy talking about old times. The time came for our goodbyes; we promised to keep in touch, and to arrange to meet again within a year. When I went back into the vicarage I found an envelope on the table. In it was a note and a cheque. The note said: *We knew all along who paid for us to go to India, hope this small cheque helps to get the organ put right. Love – Lorna and David.*' The cheque was for five thousand pounds."

Well that was Humphry's story as he told it to Ken and I, he told us to discuss it together and see if we could come up with some explanation. Apart from expressing a desire to see The Rope for ourselves we of course could not add anything. He told us that maybe someday it could be possible, he would keep it in mind.

The Room

I suppose that St Oswald's is very similar to any other rural church, an old building on a hill, with an average congregation, mostly getting on a bit in years. I suppose that the local populace, who didn't attend on a Sunday morning, had the usual idea that the folks who did were simply there for insurance purposes. Well maybe there is something in that, but what does it matter why one goes to church? – but I digress.

The vicar calls the first hymn, the people stand and the organist starts up (usually on a bum note) and proceeds to play a well-known hymn to a tune that nobody but the choir has heard of before. One can always tell that others are having difficulty, because of slight turn of heads and the slight nod in response. The bum notes by the way are always blamed on the state of the organ, hence the ongoing organ fund. The choir always sings their hearts out and cannot be criticised; it is not their faults that only one or two can sing, bless them for trying. The service proceeds and the vicar rises to give his sermon. It usually only takes a few seconds to realise the political affiliations of the vicar, and then to listen to tales of The Walls of Jericho, or The Tower of Babel. Why he is reluctant to talk about subjects that people would be interested in I can never understand, but it wouldn't matter, as most people are asleep anyway. The church committee and helpers are usually to the fore, and after the service are usually huddled together in a corner like the corporation from The Pied Piper – not to be interfered with!

I suppose all rural churches have a magazine of some sort, and I suppose they are all similar to St Oswald's. The opening predictable page from the vicar, usually a couple of very silly poems (but I have to say far superior to a lot of modern poetry), some daft quotes, and usually an article by some idiot wanting to put the world to rights, with a few adverts that nobody is interested in, and the obligatory instruction for making jam tarts or growing daisies. Church magazine editors are usually retired teachers, and ours is obviously asleep when it comes to editing the magazine, but I don't suppose it matters though, because I suspect most of them (magazines) go straight in the bin without being read. You will now realise I am sure that St Oswald's is just a normal country church probably quite similar to all the others in the country, and maybe similar to yours. I am sure you have realised that up to now this tale has been just a little tongue in cheek, but I can assure you that it is now about to become deadly serious.

I now have to take you back a number of years, to the time I became involved.

This particular Sunday morning after the service, I had just had a quick coffee, and was trying to get out of church before somebody collared me, however I wasn't quite fast enough! Why the vicar (I shall now refer to him as Walter) decided to call after me was certainly unusual, because he hadn't said anything to me apart from hello or goodbye for ages. Maybe he had had no reason to. Walter was obviously upset, and asked me if I would be kind enough to wait whilst the others had gone, to discuss something with him. I wasn't in any particular hurry, and although the old lad was a bit eccentric, I did quite like him and so I agreed. You probably are aware that many churches have what is referred to as a cold spot. St Oswald's was no exception, and I think all were aware of its presence. When everybody had gone, Walter took me to the space at the side of the vestry where our cold spot was known to be.

Covering this area was a large piece of oak trellis, which had been part of the original altar screen. It had been there as long as I could remember. Walter now told me that he had an idea that the piece of oak could probably be worth a bit, and had contacted the local joiners to see if they were interested. The boss at the joiners had duly called round was delighted with his find and made a generous donation to the church funds. It was during this inspection that the trellis was moved away from the wall.

The joiners had not been to collect it yet, and Walter now asked me to help him move it once more. When the oak was away from the wall it was plain to see that the wall had been plastered over, and an impression of a doorway was clearly visible. You will be aware that any new plaster cannot hide original access points, there is always an outline visible, however slight. Walter had the idea that I would help him to investigate. I asked him why he had chosen me. Walter had been doing some homework on me and explained his reasons. They did have a little logic I suppose, but I felt instinctively that I was the wrong person

Elgar was a large crossbred Alsatian (named after the composer). We were not very often apart, and so I decided he should accompany me to the church for our excavations. I tied him to the seat outside the church where he had been many times before, and he settled down. Walter was waiting for me and was clearly keen to get started. I asked him what he expected to find, and was he sure he wanted to continue? Yes, he wanted to continue, and he had no idea what he would find, but felt he had to go ahead. It was not difficult to chase the plaster away and after about an hour a large wooden door was visible. It was at this point that Elgar started to bark, and three gentlemen from the church committee joined us. They had seen Walter and I talking earlier, had seen my arrival with the dog, and obviously knew something was afoot. We had no alternative but to tell them the story, and that's how there came to be five of us there when we pushed the door open.

At this stage I don't want you to forget why we were here. We certainly couldn't, the cold was now really intense. Nobody was making a move to open the door, and after what seemed like an eternity Walter stepped forward, I quickly followed and together we pushed the door. It opened with just the slightest groan, and the rush of cold air coming out was unbelievable. It was obvious nobody was going any further, I certainly wasn't. After a few minutes somebody suggested my dog. I knew nothing could frighten Elgar so I went out to bring him in. It was as we were walking towards the open door that I realised all was not well with the dog, he was putting his brakes on, and as we got nearer his hackles rose, and his teeth bared. There was no way Elgar was going in that room, or so we thought! I cannot remember who was the first to notice, maybe we all did together but suddenly it grew warmer.

Then an amazing thing happened. The dog suddenly relaxed and ran into the room with his tail wagging. This was now starting to get out of hand but I wasn't about to leave him alone in the room, Walter had read my thoughts and quickly brought an extension lamp, and I entered the room closely followed by the vicar. Let me tell you straight away if you are expecting a horror story there was nothing in the room to be afraid of. It was about twelve foot by twelve foot absolutely bare, and totally clean, the walls were obviously the original stonework, the temperature was now normal, and the dog was quite happy sniffing around, his previous reaction totally forgotten.

The men from the local joiners called the next day to collect their oak trellis. Walter, in his wisdom and without any consultation, decided to have the doorway plastered up again. This was done very quickly, and Walter stacked some old church artefacts in front of the area. And so it was that things returned to normal, so normal in fact, that Walter got back to his monosyllable greetings to me, when he spoke at all. If you are still with me, we have now to move forward about two years, from our first venture into the room. The congregation had changed very little, the services were much the same. Walter was looking older and I am sure he was feeling it. I didn't feel any different, but Elgar had slowed down a great deal. What happened now was practically the same as two years earlier.

I was slipping out of church after the morning service when I heard the vicar calling me – could he have a quick word when the others had gone? Walter was clearly agitated and came straight to the point. He then proceeded to tell me that the cold spot was back again. Nobody knew of course, but Walter had been frequently checking the temperature outside the plastered doorway. I went with the vicar to the stacked artefacts. There was absolutely no doubt about it, after a second or two you could definitely feel the cold, if anyone else had noticed they certainly had not mentioned it. I asked Walter what he wanted me to do. I didn't want to believe what I heard, but he was clearly intent this time in finding out the cause of what was without doubt a very strange mystery.

And so once again, Walter and I found ourselves on Monday morning outside the plastered-up doorway with our hammers and chisels. This time we were on our own – no dog, and no committee members, when we started once again to remove the plaster. It was much easier this time, and we were soon down to the old wooden door. We both stood looking at it without speaking, and then Walter stepped forward and pushed at the door. The door slowly opened with just a slight creak, and once more the gust of icy air hit us. We both stood our ground in anticipation, and sure enough after a couple of minutes the temperature began to rise again. We already had the extension light rigged up and went into the room together.

Nothing was different.

Walter turned to me and in obvious expectation of the correct answer, asked me what we should do. I have to tell you at this point that I had spent some years in the Special Branch, Walter had somehow got to know of this, and thought quite wrongly that my ability of investigation could be useful, hence him calling me in the first place. Of course I couldn't come up with any sensible course of action. I did not want to destroy his obvious faith in me so I told him that perhaps we should get the old door out, and replace it with a smaller modern door that did not have a lock, just a catch to keep it closed. Maybe we should consider having the room plastered and painted with some pastel shade. We could have a carpet put down, and have a small table put in with a crucifix on it. Then finally the room should be blessed. I hoped that what I had said to the vicar didn't sound too silly, and was relieved when he told me his thoughts were very similar to mine.

Walter did not waste any time, and within three weeks the room was finished, and I have to say, the local decorators had done a super job. A chair had now been added, and on my first visit, when I sat down and looked around, my impression was one of warmth and peace, nothing cold or intimidating in any way. Things returned to normal again, well not quite! The vicar and I became good friends, we started to have meals together, we walked together and talked together, and I found him to be a kind, caring, and very generous old lad. He had had a very interesting life, and was quite comfortable telling me about it. I have to tell you that I also spoke of things to him that I had not spoken to anyone else about. He and Elgar also became close friends and could often be seen strolling together. My only regret was that my friendship with him had come so late. Perhaps there is a moral here.

Soon after our second entry of the room Elgar became quite ill, he was old now, and looking at me in that way that only a dog lover can recognise. I don't know why, but I decided to take him to the room. The church was usually a hive of activity, but on this day it was empty. I had to carry my old pal; he just couldn't make it on his own. I sat down on the chair and laid him gently on the floor. I was sitting there looking round thinking about what might have happened in this room, when I realised Elgar was on his feet, his tail was wagging his eyes were shining, he came up to me and licked my hand – then laid down and died. I was more certain at that time that if there was anything after death, my old pal was now experiencing it, and with a friend that would love and care for him. Of course there were tears, but I left the room knowing my dog had been happy at his passing.

With the vicar's permission, and blessing, my trusted friend was buried in a remote quiet spot in a corner of the churchyard. I managed to scrounge a small piece of the original oak trellis from the joiners and on it I had inscribed *Elgar. He has a friend in this church.*

Nobody was really aware of how it started. I know a few people had heard of my experience, but it was still surprising. It did start very slowly, almost imperceptibly, but people were beginning to use the room. It soon became frequently used and the churchwarden had to fit a vacant/engaged sign to the door to ensure the occupant was not disturbed. Some days people were limited to fifteen minutes each because of the demand, indeed there were not many days when the room was not fully used. The vicar started checking in the nicest way, to find why people were coming to our room. It seems they were visiting in bereavement, in sickness, for intercessions, for private reasons not divulged, and with pets, none of which were turned away. Nothing unpleasant was ever reported about the room, and nobody ever noticed any drop in temperature. Nobody was claiming anything miraculous about the room either; it all seemed to have ended well.

Two things now happened at the same time: I found out I had to move with my work, and Walter was becoming quite ill. On my last day in the village he asked me to go to see him in private. We had all had a little get together earlier in the week, and I was glad of this opportunity to see him alone. He was now only a shadow of the man I first knew, and I realised straight away that something was bothering him. It seemed to me that he was perfectly rational, and although upset, he spoke clearly and precisely.

I had to promise him that I would not divulge what he was about to tell me, at least until after his death. I duly promised. You need to know now, that the vicar was the only person who had the keys to the church. He would not let anyone else have them. He always opened up on time, and always locked up, no matter what time any function may have ended. His last job before locking up was always to check the room, firstly to make sure nobody was still there, and secondly to make sure the door was closed and the sign on the door said vacant. I had never seen my friend emotional before but as he started to talk tears started to form in his eyes and slowly trickle down his cheeks, I put my arm on his shoulder to comfort him until he regained his composure.

Apparently, and I know how weird this sounds when he opened the church each morning, he always found that the sign on the room door was turned round to read "engaged". He had not dared mention it to anybody and I can understand why. Obviously I could not offer any logical explanation, only to reassure him that the room did have some unexplained qualities and some things we just have to accept. At this point his eyes filled again, and he told me that every Sunday morning when he opened the church, the door to the room was ajar and there was a hassock in the church in front of the altar.

Shaking his head, he told me that this had been happening since the room was opened up and put into use. He had been unable to confide in anybody. He was clearly relieved to have unburdened himself, and with the way I had accepted it. We sat talking together until the early hours; he clearly didn't want me to go. Two weeks after I left, I heard that Walter had died suddenly in hospital. Because of pressure of work I was unable, sadly, to return for his funeral. I did intend to go back though to take my new dog Wagner to see my two old friends in the churchyard, although I have to tell you at that time I had no intentions of going in that room again.

Although I had been extremely busy since leaving the village, there were not many times when my thoughts didn't return to the strange events at St Oswald's. I cannot divulge the exact nature of my leaving, but I can tell you it was involved with a helicopter crash in Scotland. The investigation was now drawing to a close, and I was seriously thinking of taking semi-retirement. Understandably, I did not expect to be writing any more on this subject – however things change.

When we first got involved with the opening of the room at St Oswald's you will recall three gentlemen from the church committee had been present. I didn't refer to this at the time because it did not seem significant, but I became quite friendly with one of them, his name was Ken. I don't know about you, but sometimes one instinctively knows after a short time that there is a rapport. Ken turned out to be a first class bloke, and once again I found myself regretting that I had not made friends with him before. Maybe I had given the appearance of being a loner? I don't know, however you will see how important he became to me. I will tell you now (although I had never any intention of mentioning this) about the last night I spent with Walter, just before his death.

You will remember I am sure how upset he was, and that we were talking until the early hours. I realised from our discussions that Walter was a very down to earth and practical guy. What had upset him so much was the fact that he had been unable to find any normal explanation to what had happened in the church. Walter had in fact been pursuing this quest on his own since our first visit to the room. When we thought things were back to normal, they certainly were not for Walter. He had kept everything to himself apart from his requests for my assistance, and he had not divulged anything else to me until the night of our last meeting In fact instead of him actually making some progress, things had just developed, and he had fallen further behind. To come to the point, he wanted me to carry on where he left off. He told me he knew he didn't have long to live, and he would not be at rest until this mystery was sorted.

The old guy certainly put me on the spot, he knew I was going away on business and I made it clear, that I had no idea how long I would be away for. He told me I was the only one who he would talk to, and he didn't want the mystery to die with him. I could fully understand his reasoning, but how could I promise anything at the time? Not knowing if I would be away six months, or two years, I honestly didn't know.

Walter then told me that sometimes in the night when he had been unable to sleep, he would get up to make himself a cup of tea. He then told me that when glancing over at the church, which is directly overlooked by the vicarage, he had often seen a light, which looked like a candle, moving about the church. What on earth could I say? Walter was so sincere, and again tears stained his face.

The time was now about two thirty and I simply had to go, and I knew Walter should be in bed. I had no intention of making a promise to him that I couldn't keep, nor did I want to hurt him at this time. I told him not to worry and that I would be in touch. We said a tearful goodbye, and I left.

Ken and I had been corresponding quite frequently about St Oswald's and particularly how things had changed there under the new vicar. I will now tell you about the new vicar, and the changes. The new vicar, according to Ken, is a totally different character to Walter, and like the proverbial new broom was intending to sweep clean. Hearing this alarmed me a little bit; the congregation at St Oswald's needed to be treated with care and respect, if he succeeds in losing them they will not easily be replaced.

Apparently he comes over as being dogmatic, not particularly friendly, and not easy to talk to. What did worry me greatly was the next bombshell. When the new vicar found out about the room and its popularity, he apparently went mad. His immediate reaction according to Ken, was to inform the church committee that the room would be closed henceforth, he said that anybody who needed to use that room for whatever reason could just as well use the church, emphasising that's what the church was there for. He apparently stated further, that no animals would be allowed in the church. When the history of the room was explained to him, he apparently scoffed and intimated he had never heard anything so ridiculous.

So it came to be that the room was once again sealed. Not by plaster this time, but it was emptied, a stout external lock fitted and some large heavy articles placed in front of the door. The natives were not happy, and Ken wanted me to go down to talk to him about the problem. I had been waiting for a reason to return, and now my work in Scotland was over, I was happy to agree. The next day after a pleasant drive down from Scotland I arrived at Ken's little place near to St Oswald's. I explained to him that before we had our discussion I wanted to go over to the church. Ken understood, and so after a welcome cup of tea, and some small talk, I set off for the church with Wagner. I didn't know the current policy on dogs in the churchyard so decided to leave him tied to the seat outside.

The scene that greeted me was unbelievable! Elgar's oak plaque was clean and the small grave tidy, but next to it, and remember we are talking about a remote spot here, was dear Walter's grave. The thing that reduced me to tears was the simple inscription "Walter, he had a friend in the church also". Nothing more. I subsequently found out that this was Walter's wish before he died, to be laid beside Elgar.

It was while I was wiping my face, that I realised someone had walked up behind me. When I turned I realised it was a reverend gentleman and I assumed he was the new vicar. He inquired about the grave, and was most surprised to hear it was his predecessor buried there, he genuinely didn't know.

He then noticed Elgar's grave and commented on the unusual inscriptions, I didn't enlighten him about Elgar, but explained that he had died first, and to keep things simple, explained his inscription referred to the vicar. With regards to Walter's inscription, I was not privy to the requests of the vicar, but told him Elgar was a dear friend. I didn't give him any time to dwell on what I had just said, but asked him straight out if Ken and I could see him as soon as possible to discuss an important issue. I explained that I had been at the church some time ago, had been away on business and had just returned. His response was quite normal, he would be glad to meet us, and he was pleased to see me back.

We met later that evening and proceeded to tell the whole story in detail from start to finish. Humphry (the new vicar) did not interrupt nor did he show any emotion. We finished and waited; after what seemed like an eternity he spoke. In his opinion there was obviously a simple explanation to the room, and we had all missed it, but it had to be simple. With regards to Walter's comments on the door sign being turned round, the door being found open, the hassock in front of the altar, and ghostly visions at night, these were purely tricks of the mind of an old sick man. He would be interested to hear our views, after some very serious consideration, and investigation.

Two days later Ken and I met over a drink in the private room of the hostelry where I was staying. Ken wanted me to start. I hoped that didn't mean that he had expected me to come up with the answers. I explained that I had explored the history of St Oswald's in some detail. There had in fact been a religious building on this site since records began nine hundred years ago, however it was thought that the building was a thousand years old. This meant that its life span covered all the turmoil that the church suffered. Among these events were the black-death, the inquisition, the reformation, and the civil wars. What this told us I did not know, nor did I particularly want to go down the path of tortured bodies, sealed in buildings, awaiting somebody else to liberate them centuries later.

Ken's route would be the best bet I was thinking. His was the structural path. He then told me that he had discussed the problem with an architect friend of his. The architect had told him that in old stone buildings, if there is no circulation of air possible in a room, that is if the area is sealed for some reason – but there is any access however slight from beneath the building into the room, then it could indeed become very cold. Much colder in fact than the normal air temperature. This would explain we both thought, the sudden equalisation of temperature, following the initial cold blast on opening the door to the room. We both relaxed a little.

This of course was the answer, and seemed to settle most of the questions; maybe the new vicar was correct after all. We arranged to meet him the next day, and explained our findings. His only question was to ask why we hadn't tried to find the sensible solution straight away. He wasn't at all patronising and stated that now the room would be sealed, so there could be no air flow from below. He also would wager that there would be no more temperature variations. With a grin on his face he offered to place a bet to that effect. Both Ken and I declined to take his offer.

It was perhaps two months later than Ken called me in Scotland I had just sewn up all my lose ends and sold my small cottage, where I had originally intended to stay. (Just let's say it was my yearning for Yorkshire and dislike of carnivorous midges that made me change my mind) and I was ready to move south to look for somewhere permanent. Well I don't think there is need to tell you what Ken said in detail. Humphry had been to see him, yes, the wall outside the room was getting colder.

The new vicar had suspected it over a number of weeks, he had been removing his barricade at night unknown to anybody else, and checking. He asked Ken if he would contact me to see if we could all meet to discuss it. He certainly didn't want to keep anything to himself as Walter had, he explained. And so it was two days later Ken, Humphry, and I met in the hostelry where I once again had booked in. This of course put paid to our theory, i.e. no air flow into the room from beneath, the fact that the door was now unsealed. The theory was well and truly in tatters.

For the first time Humphry looked a little shaken. There was nothing now I wanted to add, and Ken felt exactly the same. Consequently the meeting dissolved into chit-chat, and a short time later we parted. Humphry had assured us he knew what to do, and neither of us decided to ask him what his intentions were. Two weeks later the job was done. The room no longer existed. The vestry now embraced the area of the old room, the connecting, and inner stone walls had been removed. The extended vestry was all newly decorated, it was light and airy and of course there were no doors, just drapes which would be always open, apart from pre and post services times.

We are now up to date. I have bought a cottage near the church, Ken and I are still best friends and Humphry is often seen out with us. He has also had some work done! On the left side of the church, (the part overlooked from the vicarage), a small chapel has been added. The table, chair, and crucifix from the room have been put in the chapel along with other seating. Anybody can use the chapel in private for whatever reason, and any animals are welcome with their owners on Wednesdays.

In the small chapel is a plaque, which reads "This chapel is dedicated to the loving memory of Walter, and his friend Elgar". By the way, Humphry confided in Ken and I that he still finds a hassock in front of the altar on some mornings. Fortunately he hasn't asked us to investigate, he just tells us he thinks it is Walter getting his own back!

I cannot finish the story without telling you this: Wagner has a habit of disappearing from time to time, I won't tell you where I always find him! But I will tell you he is the only dog that Humphry will allow in the church and grounds unaccompanied!

I suspect Wagner knows something we are not meant to know.

The Female Bully

Maureen and Zoe were two lovely girls. They were thirteen, sporty and academically talented. They lived near to each other and were seldom apart. Activities after school for them, included music, dance and athletics. It would not be fair to say that their friendship excluded any others, they were indeed very popular both with other children and with the staff, however their friendship was obviously very strong and nobody had challenged it.

Audrey had been at the school about six months, and it had to be said, she had been making a nuisance of herself. She was a tall, well-built girl, not particularly bright, and not keen on sport. She was known to be a bully, and delighted in putting the "frighteners" on other children. It was suspected also, that she was not too honest. Maureen and Zoe were certainly aware of Audrey and her reputation, but so far had not had any problems. That was about to change.

Audrey had been warned of her behaviour, her mother had been asked to attend school, but she turned out to be uncooperative and aggressive. Audrey's attitude did not improve and she now turned her attention on Maureen and Zoe. First it was proximity, then staring, then verbal contact. The next stage was threats and demands – this was apparently her modus operandi. Maureen and Zoe tolerated Audrey, and tried not to show any concern from her unwanted attention, they ignored her threats and demands, and knew that they were taking the heat off some other girl. It was one evening after school things turned nasty.

While taking their usual short cut through the wood to their homes Audrey jumped out, knocking them both to the ground. She demanded money and warned them of the consequences of non-compliance. It turned out that our bully had a nice little income going from children too frightened to talk. Maureen and Zoe were not hurt, and agreed to pay the going rate. When Audrey had gone, Maureen said, "What are we going to do about her then? She is beginning to annoy me."

"Me too," Zoe answered. "Let's have a talk about the options, we obviously have to proceed with care, but I think we should be able to make her see the error of her ways."

"I am sure we will," said Maureen, with a touch of humour in her voice.

Maureen and Zoe had arranged to stay that evening at Zoe's parent's house. Professor Wright, Zoe's dad, had just arrived home when the two friends got there. After chatting for a few minutes they asked to be excused to do their homework, and made their way to Zoe's room.

The homework they had in mind, and indeed started, was not of the school type. As they approached the school the next morning, neither of them seemed surprised to see Audrey's mum getting out of a car outside the school gates.

"I wonder what she is doing here?" said Maureen.

"Yes I wonder too," said Zoe. Both girls had just a hint of a smile ….

At the end of morning assembly, the headmistress asked the assembled children to join in a prayer for Audrey. She had apparently been taken ill the previous night and was now in hospital. When the assembly was over Maureen and Zoe were asked to go the Headmistress's office.

"Did you see Audrey last night girls?" was the first question. Maureen and Zoe looked at one another, but neither replied.

"Girls this is serious, Audrey's mother said that you two were the last to see her last night, I must know what happened."

After a brief pause Zoe explained what had happened on their way home from school.

"Is that the last time you saw her, now tell the truth."

"Yes it is," said Zoe. "My dad was in all night and he knows we didn't go out."

"Well, Audrey told her mother you two did something to her, and she has been to the police, they are coming round to your house tonight Zoe, will your mum and dad be there?"

"Yes they will."

"Okay, that's all for now."

On their way back to class Maureen said, "Well it obviously worked."

"It certainly seems to have," said Zoe. They both smiled.

Professor Wright was a research scientist. His field was the human brain. He worked at the local university. Maureen's father was a solicitor. The two men were friends and were having a quiet drink when the police arrived. Maureen and Zoe told their story from their first acquaintance with Audrey, until they left her the previous night. Zoe's dad confirmed the time they arrived home, and that they never left the house after that. Maureen's father wanted to know what it was all about.

The police inspector then said, "Audrey went to the fish shop at about nine last night. When she arrived home she was distressed, and told her mum that you two girls had done something to her. Shortly afterwards the doctor was called and she had to be taken to hospital. The strange thing is, they don't seem to know what is wrong with her, and she cannot speak now."

"We didn't go out last night or see her after we got home from school, so how could we have done anything?" responded Maureen.

"Well I just had to ask, you know how it is, sir," he said, addressing Maureen's father, who he knew.

"Yes, I know how it is alright," he replied, without any expression.

The policemen left, and the conversation that followed was about Audrey and what could be wrong with her. Shortly afterwards Maureen walked out of the house with Zoe while their fathers were still talking.

"How long shall we give her then," said Zoe quietly.

"I think a week should just about do it," replied Maureen. "Let's hope the next bit works okay." They were both still smiling when Maureen's dad came out of the house and opened the car door for his daughter.

Professor Wright was hardly ever consulted on a clinical basis. He had written several books on the function of the brain, which were held to be definitive. He was more concerned now with research and lecturing. He was therefore not a little surprised to find himself summoned to the general hospital. The case of a young lady patient was presented to him by the consultant neurosurgeon. She had apparently all the normal vital signs, did not appear to be ill in the normal sense, but had a crazy electroencephalogram, or EEG. She appeared to have lost the power of communication. Professor Wright did not mind his regime being interfered with if the case was interesting, and this one seemed to be just that. He discussed the patient at length with the consultants, and examined the EEG results with great excitement. This sort of patient was what his job was all about.

Professor Wright was then taken through to the small side ward where the patient was. She looked like any other child of her age, and it was only when he spotted her name that alarm bells started to ring.

"Audrey Smith?" said the professor. "Is this the young lady from the girl's high school who was brought in a couple of nights ago?"

"Yes Professor," said the consultant. "This is she."

"I am sorry," said the professor, "but for ethical reasons I cannot continue with this case. My daughter and her friend have somehow been implicated in this affair, and the police have been involved. There is no way I can be involved at this stage. I am sure you understand."

"I was relying on you sir, you are the foremost authority on this kind of case. If I have to operate, I will need to be told what to do."

"Well I certainly won't be telling you my friend," said the professor. "But let me say, if you wish to discuss an anonymous case with me privately at my home, that is a different thing. You may wish also to discuss an MR scan of a certain brain – I will say no more, good morning to you."

It was raining so hard that the children all stayed in school over the break period. Maureen and Zoe had placed a pin in the centre of a lab table and were trying to make it move without touching it. Soon a group of girls were round the table wanting to know what was going on. Maureen explained that she had seen a Russian lady on television make a pin move without touching it. She suggested to the girls that if they all stood round the table and willed the pin to move together it just might work – all the girls eagerly stood round.

"Okay," said Zoe who had taken up a position directly opposite Maureen, "when I say 'go', all concentrate hard on trying to move the pin. But you must stay completely quiet."

The room had not been so quiet for a long time.

After a couple of minutes the pin started to move, almost imperceptibly at first, but definite movement. Then it jumped off the table a couple of inches. It was at this point that screams and giggles started, as you would expect.

One girl said, "It's done with thin cotton."

Another girl said, "I have seen it done with a magnet, it's just a trick like the Ouija board."

Yet another girl said, "My parents told me the Ouija board is not a trick, and that I should never get involved with it, I don't like things like that."

It was time for the girls to return to class. Whilst they were walking the short distance to their History classroom, Maureen looked at Zoe and said quietly, "Thin cotton – magnets." Both girls were once again grinning.

It was a few days later when the neurosurgeon called at Professor Wright's home. He had with him the latest information about a patient. The professor had the means to link through to the imaging department at the hospital, and was able to view the latest EEG readout, and to view the MR scan results. After a few minute the professor said.

"It looks for all the world as if this patient had a stroke, or some heavy blow to the head, but clearly this is not the case. There is no pressure in the brain, and the fact that all other signs are normal would rule out stroke. The EEG results tell me however that the brain is still in flux, it almost seems as if someone has tapped into this brain with a computer and lowered the security level, similarly to how one would set a the security level on a computer. The brain is quite normal and trying to operate, but it is being restricted. There is nothing to be gained from operating on this patient, because there is nothing wrong with the brain itself."

"What should the treatment be then Professor?" asked the now worried-looking consultant.

"That's a difficult one to answer, I have only seen this once before – that was the result of an hypnotism demonstration which went wrong. In that particular case normal function returned in about three weeks. I think you will just have to observe and wait."

Maureen and Zoe were just leaving the headmistresses office where they had asked to be able to visit Audrey. The Head had been asking if any girl would visit Audrey – but there had been no offers. She was delighted then to receive this offer, and contacted Audrey's mum. There were no objections from her mum and it was arranged they would go that afternoon. The doctors had already explained to Audrey's mother that because Maureen and Zoe were the two last girls that Audrey had seen before she became ill, she had associated them with her problem, it was as simple as that. Audrey's mum had accepted this explanation and acted quite normally when the two girls arrived. Audrey was not able to communicate in any way, and the girls were happy when her mum left them to go for a cigarette. Zoe then took Audrey's hand in hers.

"If you can understand me Audrey, squeeze my hand." Zoe felt pressure on her hand.

"You have brought this situation on yourself Audrey, you know that don't you?" Zoe again felt a slight pressure on her hand.

"Only you can cure this problem, the doctors cannot help you. You will have to convince yourself that there will be no more bullying at school, you must be kind and understanding to all the other girls and to the teachers. Only if you promise yourself this will you get better. Maureen and I will help you, will you promise?" Zoe felt a tighter squeeze of her hand this time.

Maureen then said, "Audrey, if you go back on what you have just promised, you will be ill again and may not get better next time, do you fully understand?" Audrey understood all right.

That evening Maureen and Zoe were busy working, but as before it wasn't schoolwork they were doing. Four weeks later Audrey was well enough to return to school.

Just before Audrey was due to return to school, Zoe and Maureen were having a conversation.

"I don't want to be involved with this anymore Zoe," said Maureen. "We just don't know enough about it, and really we should be concentrating fully on our school work now."

"Yes you are right, maybe some time in the future?"

"Yes maybe."

That evening before Zoe's dad came home, the two girls went into his library and carefully returned two books onto the shelves.

One was called *Control by Telepathy is Possible* and the other *Experiments with Telekinesis*. Both books were written by Zoe's dad.

Audrey became a model pupil, she did well academically, and also at sports. She became well liked by the other pupils and staff, and went on to university. Maureen and Zoe went on to medical school; they both gained excellent medical degrees and quickly became consultants. They both now work with Professor Wright doing neurological research.

Abject Terror

I had been posted to RAF Gatesbury in the south of England. Gatesbury was one of the main radio training schools. "Radio" embraced wireless, radar, instrument landing systems and other aircraft electronics.

I had just finished basic training and had been sent here to learn before being let loose on aircraft on an operational unit. Most arrivals were like me, Aircraftsmen 2nd class (the lowest one can be). The camp had to be guarded, and after 5pm the airmen whose job it was to guard the camp all knocked off for the day. (These guys would have been RAF police, or maybe RAF regiment). It was then up to the guys on the various courses to cover the guard duties. Fortunately Gatesbury being a large camp, meant guard duty didn't come round too often – which was good because everyone hated it.

My first duty eventually arrived. Uniforms had to be spot on, everything had to gleam, boots were like mirrors – even then we knew something would be picked up at the inspection which preceded every guard duty. I found myself on the ten till one shift, not too bad, if all went well I could get some sleep. The guard was stood down at seven in the morning. There was this building; we marched past it frequently on the way to our lectures, and also to the camp cinema. The building was wooden structured like all the rest – but it was always empty. Rumour had it that it was haunted.

Each guard was issued with a torch and a truncheon, and was given an area to patrol. Guard patrols could be (and were) checked by the NCO in charge and also the orderly officer. There was no skiving. I commenced my duty at 10pm, winter was approaching and it was cold and miserable. Initially there were other airmen around, leaving the NAAFI, cinema, and other places of recreation, but soon it was very quiet. Walking round a military establishment at night with lots of buildings and dim lights and shadows is not in itself very pleasant. When one knows however that on your patrol is a place that is claimed to be haunted, all sorts of silly things go on in your mind.

What had happened in this place? Why was it always deserted? Why didn't anyone tell us about it? The building was now in my sight I gripped my baton tightly and walked on. I deliberately didn't look at the building but increased my pace to get past as quickly as possible. I knew at once – there was no mistake, the temperature had dropped significantly. I glanced at the building – nothing obvious, and as soon as I passed the temperature returned to normal. I had to pass this place three times on my duty (not from choice) and each time I had the same experience. After my duty ended the sergeant asked me if all was in order. I told him about the building – he just replied that all was in order then. I didn't get any sleep that night, and it was a very tired airman that attended his lectures the next morning.

My next guard duty about four weeks later was at the aircraft pound about three miles from the main camp. This pound had an assortment of aircraft from the war. They were mostly bombers. I can remember the Lancaster, Halifax, Blenheim, Wellington and Mosquito and there were probably others. Some aircraft still had functioning equipment and these were used for training purposes. We were encouraged to look in all the aircraft to get an idea what conditions would have been like for the crews.

Many questions and answers were given; it was a very rewarding experience.

Walking round the aircraft during the day with others, and walking round in the dark on one's own is a very different matter. This was a large area, and large aircraft at night look rather frightening especially when silhouetted. Noises seem to come from everywhere – lights seem to shine from everywhere, especially when the torch was switched on. I didn't like it. I had no idea really why this area was being guarded. There was a large perimeter fence and I couldn't really see why anyone would want to break in to a pound with old disabled WW2 aircraft.

Something made me stop in front of a large bomber. I slowly scanned the plane from back to front with my torch, when my torch beam illuminated the cockpit the adrenaline rush nearly took my head off – looking down at me was a grotesque image of a face. I wanted to turn and run but I was riveted to the spot, my heart was pounding – I was suffering total and absolute terror. Then a hand slowly rose into view the fingers spread as if clawing at the window of the cockpit.

After what seemed like an eternity but what was in reality would have been only a short time I managed to tear myself away from this horror. The night was cold and frosty, I had a greatcoat on and although I tried to run, I found it impossible. Trying to run round large bombers in the dark in a heavy coat is not to be recommended. Eventually I arrived at the guard post. Now please ask yourselves how you would have handled this. Remember in those days there were no mobile methods of communication.

The sergeant of the guard took one look at me and at once knew all was not right. Over a pot of tea I told him as clearly as possible what I had just seen. He told me it must have been a trick of the light. The other two guards who were present were noticeably disturbed by my story. I didn't want to go back, but couldn't believe what I was hearing when I insisted that the sergeant come back with me. One guard was left in the post and the three of us set off. In my terror I wasn't at all sure where I was heading. There must have been forty aircraft in the pound. I remembered I had dropped my baton and asked the other two to look for it – we now had three torches. After about ten minutes the other guard spotted the baton and called out; so now there were three of us under the front of the bomber.

The sergeant asked me to show him exactly what I did, and where I had shone the torch. I started at the back and slowly shone the beam up the fuselage and on to the cockpit. There was nothing there – and then very slowly the face appeared. If anything it was more grotesque, the mouth open and twisted – the arm and hand once again slowly appeared and seemed to claw at the window. The sergeant was unable to move, my fellow guard was being sick. I cannot put here what was said – I leave you to imagine.

When the sergeant had composed himself as much as was possible, he sent the other guard back to the post to ring for the orderly officer. I was much braver now with someone else there and feeling somewhat vindicated, I suggested we investigate further. The sergeant wasn't over keen, but reluctantly agreed. We ran a boarding ladder into position and the sergeant climbed up, I was shining both torches. What happened next I will not forget until my dying day. The sergeant opened the cockpit door, and I shone the two torches inside from my position on the ground. A figure suddenly appeared in the doorway – the face now caught in my upward shining torch beams more grotesque than ever, the hand and arm raised with claw like fingers extended. The sergeant passed out and fell from the ladder. I held my torch on the spectre, which took a step as if to descend the ladder – and then the spectre collapsed on to ground beside the sergeant.

My brain was now starting to function and I realised this was no spectre – it was a fellow airman and a quick check told me he was in a desperate condition. He was in a state of hypothermia and deadly cold. The temperature inside the aircraft must have been akin to a fridge. The sergeant was starting to come round, and I quickly got his and my greatcoats off and over the airman. Shortly afterwards the orderly officer arrived, the other guard had had the sense to ask for an ambulance, and not knowing clearly what was wrong, a medical officer had also attended the scene. It must have looked like a battleground when they arrived. The airman from the plane was rushed away in the ambulance; the sergeant was helped back to the guardroom. When we were all reasonably composed the orderly officer debriefed us. I have never known this happen before, but the guard was stood down, and the reserve guard was called in.

By way of explanation:-

That afternoon a group of airmen had been brought down to the aircraft pound to do the rounds of the planes. Somehow (and this was never established) an airman was left in a plane and unable to get out. The lorry had loaded up the airmen and returned to camp without missing anyone. When the lorry had got back to camp it was teatime, there was no check on personnel, after tea – leisure time, and then bedtime. It was quite common to go to bed and to sleep with a few beds vacant – nobody asked questions and they were always occupied in the morning. It would then have been the next morning at first lecture before the airman was found to be missing.

The guy in the aircraft only had a thin denim overall over his battledress, totally inadequate for a frosty winter evening. I had warm underclothes, shirt, long sleeved jersey, battle dress and large military overcoat – I was still cold. His grotesque appearance was because of the intense cold he was suffering from. His right arm was raised and fingers extended because he was trying to hold himself upright by an overhead strap so he could be seen, a very wise decision as it turned out.

The guy made a complete recovery. He had though damaged his vocal chords with shouted, and was unable to speak for a number of days. The poor airman didn't know that there was no one to hear his cries.

The sergeant made a complete recovery. I however did not. It is easy to understand when one has the explanation – but I sometimes still see that face in the cockpit window, and go cold to this day.

I eventually graduated from RAF Gatesbury and was posted to a Navigator training school. I there worked on the systems I had trained on at Gatesbury, in Vampire and Venom jet fighters.

RAF Gatesbury no longer exists. It seems it would be very difficult to recognise anything of the camp now, and nature has reclaimed it. Apparently a plaque has been placed outside what was the camp. It pays tribute to all the personnel who worked and trained there before, during and after the war.

I recently came across a guy on the internet who had written an article about his RAF service, I pricked my ears up when he mentioned RAF Gatesbury. I contacted him and we exchanged a few memories. In one of his messages he said, "Did you ever go past the haunted building while doing guard duty?"

An Unexpected Break

Fortunately, or so I thought, I would make it without too much stress. I was now only about five miles from base, and although the weather had turned quite nasty, at least I was on ground I knew. Five miles was no problem to me, even though I was tired, wet, cold, and beginning to feel hungry. In fact I didn't feel any different to what I had felt a hundred times before; a nice feeling of anticipating of what was to come, after a super day walking the moors: a hot bath, nice meal, and a few drinks.

I must tell you that usually I have at least one comrade with me, but on this occasion, because they had all dropped out for some reason, it had to be on my own, or not at all. I chose to come alone. This should not have created any trouble for me; after all, I had walked the moors plenty of times before, without any cause for concern. I could now see the lights of the village in the valley. At least I could when the clouds cleared, as they frequently but briefly did. I had just started to ascend the last climb of maybe a mile, before the final drop down to the right and journey's end.

At first I thought it was a trick of the fast-fading light. Normally I would have been back before this time, but being out alone it is too easy to loiter and take longer over the route. I soon realised it was no trick. Indeed there was someone walking towards me, maybe now three hundred yards away. My first reaction was: why on earth would anybody be venturing up onto open moorland at this late hour, and in this rapidly deteriorating weather? I surely was puzzled. I have to make clear that the village I was now nearing was not my village, but just a stopping off point for the night. I was not a stranger there, but I was only really known in the small pub where I was booked in for the night.

What happened now was stupid. Instead of watching where I was treading, my eyes were being drawn to the approaching figure, and in the bad light I missed my footing, and fell sideways about fifteen feet down an embankment. I landed with a thud on some rocks. The pain was intense and I knew instantly that I had broken my right leg: I could feel the protruding bone. At this point I must have become unconscious.

The next thing that I was aware of was standing at the back of what I can only describe as a large, white cathedral. I could not do it justice by trying to describe it. It was high, and the ceiling was painted in the most wonderful designs and colours. The inside walls were of smooth white marble carved in stunning designs. Music was being played like I have never heard it before. I couldn't believe the quality of sound coming from the organ. I looked around me in awe. I then let my eyes drift towards the front. All I could see was a vivid, bright white light. The smell as I slowly walked down the centre aisle was indescribable: can you imagine the perfume of freesias, wallflowers, stocks, and other scented flowers all intermingled?

I only now became aware of someone at my side. I turned to look at him; he smiled and asked me if I knew where I was. He confirmed that my answer was correct, but quickly told me that my visit would only be a fleeting one. He told me that I was very privileged to be where I was, and that very few people had been here as casual visitors. We could only get so near to the white light. There was no obvious barrier, but nevertheless our progress was halted. My companion explained that we were nearing a very special place, and very few could proceed any further. I had to ask him if this was the same light that people claimed to see in near death experiences on earth. He explained that indeed it is, and said that many people had seen the light in anticipation, but had been a little premature, and had to return to their bodies. He also went on to tell me that the people who had had these experiences had no fear of death. I knew this to be true. I had to ask him the obvious question: Why had I been brought here? He just smiled at me.

I asked him how long I would be away. He then went on to tell me that time did not exist here, that I should not worry about it, but just try to remember as much as possible about my visit. We walked to the side of the building and out through a large door. He again reminded me to remember as much detail as possible of what I was about to see.

After my first footstep outside I was literally stopped in my tracks. I will try to describe the scene but it is difficult to do it justice. First of all, the colours that greeted my eyes were like nothing I had seen before: the intensity, the depth, the range. I swear there were colours I had not seen before. My companion beckoned me forward. To say we were walking would be inaccurate. I seemed to have a walking action, but yet seemed to be gliding. The scenery, as we progressed, was amazing, with beautiful fields, hills, lakes, and trees. I then began to notice birds and hear their songs. Then animals started to appear in the fields and hills, all different kinds. I couldn't believe what I was seeing.

My companion turned and told me I was trying too hard, and to relax a little. He explained that on this occasion I would only get a flavour of the wonders that were here. He then went on to tell me that people who are here to stay very quickly learn to control their curiosity, and make progress slowly. He continued, "Because this place is eternal, there is no need for time. When people on earth who believe in an afterlife try to imagine what it is like they usually hope that they will be reunited with loved ones, and that it will be a place of peace with no worry or stress. Well, that is reasonable to hope for, and understandable, but it doesn't scratch the surface of the wonders that are waiting."

The multitude of scenes and ideas were getting very difficult for me to take in now, and my companion was certainly aware of this fact, because he turned to me and said, "Perhaps you would like to ask a question."

The host of questions that I would have liked to ask had now dissolved in an instant; I was frantically trying to think of maybe one question that others given the chance would ask. I decided to ask him this: "Why is there such appalling suffering on earth?"

This was his reply: "Man was given free choice, to run life on Earth as he chose. Do you think that anyone here would allow such suffering, if they had any control? A human lifetime is but a blink of an eye from here, and you have to believe me that everyone will answer for his or her actions on earth. The spirit is pure energy and cannot be destroyed or altered in any way. At death it will contain every detail of your life. All souls of human beings head towards the white light for judgement, and – let's be sensible here – you all have the same chance, the knowledge is there for everyone. The rules of the earthly journey are clear. If people choose to ignore them, or distort them, then so be it. Likewise, anybody who uses fancy or eloquent words, to try to proclaim what they may want to be true, rather than what they know to be true, should take great care. I can tell you The Governor is not an easy option."

There were obviously other questions I wanted to ask, indeed they were now coming to mind thick and fast. Many answers to my unasked questions were being shown to me though. For instance, I saw groups of people who were obviously families with dogs and cats and other pets. I saw young couples together and elderly people with young people. I saw people participating in all kinds of games and sports. Once again my mind was having trouble taking it all in. The next moment we were on our own again, walking on a beautiful beach. This indeed was a place that I would like to explore in detail, but that was obviously not going to be the case as we were now approaching the building, and I knew instinctively that my time was fast running out. When we entered, it was filled with wonderful music. We sat down and listened, I could have stayed listening forever.

"Before I send you on your way, have you a last question."

I couldn't think, and blurted out, "Are there such things as angels?"

"Most certainly my friend, I am an angel."

He then bent over to me, whispered something in my ear, and gently pushed me towards the bright light. This time there was no barrier, and I started to enter the brilliant glow. The light was getting more intense, and I was forced to close my eyes. However, just before they were shut I could see a figure looking down at me. He put his hand out and touched my forehead

I awoke at this point to find the couple who run the pub in the village standing over me. Mike was touching my forehead and asking how I felt.

It took me a few minutes to get myself together, and I asked him what had happened. He told me that I had had an accident on the moor and that my companion had carried me down from the moor to the pub. He also told me that he was sure my leg was broken when I was carried in, and that he wanted to phone for an ambulance. My friend then told him that his name was Angelo and that he was a doctor, and he would check me over first. Apparently, he was with me for about fifteen minutes.

Well, if my leg was broken up on the moor, (and I know for sure that it was), it most certainly was not broken now. Mike was also looking down at my leg and he said he couldn't believe it either. He then said that my friend Angelo had to leave, but he had told him that I would soon be okay again, and that he would be in touch with me, and I shouldn't worry about anything.

Mike asked me if he should ring for an ambulance, but I was feeling fine now, so I declined his offer. Soon afterwards I began to think of what had occurred, and what people would say when I told them of it. I know some would claim it has just been a dream. Well, okay, it may have been, but it was certainly the most realistic dream I have ever had.

I mused it would have taken me at least an hour to get to the pub, under normal circumstances. Mike and I worked out that from the time of my accident, to waking up in the pub was no more than an hour.

I obviously had to be extracted from the spot I had fallen into, and after having my leg strapped. Then, I was presumably carried to the village. The shorter route across country was one shunned by hikers. It consisted of a steep scree, a large boggy area, and then a river crossing: clearly not to be attempted whilst carrying a twelve stone person over your shoulder. Then my injuries had presumably been attended to.

If Angelo had taken fifteen minutes to check and prepare me on the moor, (and he was in the pub room with me for a further fifteen minutes), then this would have left no more than thirty minutes to get me from the moor to the village. Clearly this was not humanly possible. Remember we are talking of about five miles of uneven terrain, in poor light and bad weather, plus my rucksack was also brought down with me. My heavenly experience seemed to have taken place over at least two hours.

Although the questions I asked were reasonable, I would have asked different questions had I been prepared. The answers to my questions don't necessarily match what I would have expected. Heaven was not as I would have expected either. I had never met my Heavenly companion on earth, yet he told Mike he was my friend, and that his name was Angelo. Why was he walking towards me on the moor?

It is a while now since that day on the moor, and my life has returned to normal. I still frequently think about my experience on that stormy evening, and dream or not, I can tell you I have critically examined my lifestyle.

Oh, by the way, I told you that just before I left the cathedral my companion whispered something in my ear. He said, "When you return to earth, be sure to look in the front pocket of your rucksack." I remembered later that same evening while still in bed. I opened the pocket to find a small piece of paper. On it was written: *How's the leg? Angel-o.*

The Worst Nightmare Ever

Realising that it was a nightmare, it was comforting to know that waking up would be no problem, having woken myself from such dreams many times before. These creatures were after me with the box. Running away from them down a road it was getting increasingly difficult for me to progress, my feet were beginning to feel extremely heavy, seeking escape from the creatures. I ran into a house and knew immediately it was the wrong thing to do. There were six people in the room, all dressed in black, they each had very long white faces and stared at me but said nothing. Dragging myself to some stairs in the room corner, it was not difficult for me to detect a feeling of great evil, this feeling was so strong it caused a reluctance for me to proceed further, but the creatures with the box were gaining and the desire to get away from them was now absolutely overwhelming. Being petrified with fear, it had now become a major effort to move at all. Dragging myself agonisingly up the stairs, and breathing with great difficulty it seemed enough was enough, and it seemed about the right time to wake myself up.

My situation now was truly terrifying; always able to wake myself from nightmares before – but what came fairly easy previously, was not working now. I was tossing, turning, groaning, and fighting for consciousness, it didn't come, this was indeed deep trouble for me. The creatures with the box were now starting to climb the stairs; no way could I bring myself to look behind me.

The bridge was high; there was nowhere to walk – only iron girders. Being a sufferer from acrophobia this situation was agonising. Under the bridge was a torrent of water, which was turning into a giant whirlpool directly underneath me. Edging along the girders I knew the creatures were after me with the box, I just had to keep going. There was a gap in the bridge but it was too wide to get across. I have never known such fear, and tried again to wake myself, but without success. In desperation I attempted the leap across the gap, didn't make it and started to fall. Just before hitting the whirlpool I found myself on a high wall.

This was the most frightening thing I have ever experienced. The wall had only very small handholds, and as I got higher the handholds were getting smaller. Spiders totally screw me up, imagine my reaction then when I looked down to see swarms of spiders climbing up the wall after me. Hovering above me were the creatures with the box. I was paralysed with indescribable horror, the spiders were now crawling over me. I was now physically sick, wet through, and sobbing.

The large room at first glance didn't seem to offer anything to be afraid of. I tried to relax a little – but then the room door opened and this evil looking man walked in. To my shame I realised that I was completely naked, and on turning round found the room was full of people. Being unable to move, covering myself was not possible; then the people in the room started to prod and touch me, I was distraught, but worse was to come. The evil looking one started to read from this book. He was reading all the things I have done in my life, and after each passage he hit me with a large whip. I begged him not to read anymore but he just smirked at me and continued. The pain of what he was reading out, was far worse than the stinging pain of the whip; being whipped for an hour at least, both back and front, my body was cut to ribbons. About this time, I started wishing for death. Alas it wasn't going to be that easy.

Who was this young boy walking by my side? I had never seen him before, but knew instinctively that his safety rested with me. To my dread I realised the creatures with the box were after me again. Not wanting to frighten the boy but realising we had to speed up, progress once more became difficult. Glancing round, it was plain to see the creatures were gaining on us. How much more could one be expected to take? I pushed the boy on ahead and turned to face my pursuers. Whilst I was turned round the boy was dragged away from me, and a fire had started between myself and the creatures with the box; turning to look for the boy, I was just in time to see him being pulled away before the fire encircled me. The scene as I peered through the smoke after the boy was one of torture both for the boy and myself, he had been stretched out on a tree and was being nailed to the tree through his hands. He was screaming for me, I was crawling through the fire to get to him, and being burnt alive.

My raw flesh from the whipping in the room was now burnt from me, pain could no longer reach me, torment must surely be behind me. Wrong! My feet tightly bound, hands tied painfully behind my back I was suspended over a hole in thick ice. Always having had a great fear of drowning, or being trapped under water, I suffered the agony of being lowered into the icy water. This was it – breathing would let water into my lungs, I would end it. I couldn't suffer anymore, I was finished. As soon as the unbelievable cold hit my shredded body I tried to breathe. To my dread, this action was denied me, lower and lower into the icy depth with lungs bursting, unable to take in water, I remember this large slimy thing swimming towards me.

The middle of the desert meant no relief from my nightmare, having nothing to drink, and no clothing to protect me from the blistering sun. My body was half burnt, and half frostbitten. The sun was thawing my frozen parts and once again I was experiencing pain beyond pain. I was crawling aimlessly in the sand, which was in my wounds; and in my nose, ears and mouth. Insects were beginning to crawl over my shredded body; snakes were sidewinding towards me. What was the point? Nothing could end this – I was destined for eternal torture.

Finding myself on a country road seemed miraculous, normality seemed to have returned, my body was clothed, no pain or injury plagued me. Birds were singing; the sun was gently warming. I seemed to be through my nightmare and into a normal dream. Just down the road was a small stream with crystal clear water gurgling over smooth stones. I headed towards it in anticipation of drinking deeply; my whole body was demanding water. Just about twenty yards from the stream, I noticed this sign in the middle of the road. It said: "Road Ahead Closed. Please return via your outward route." I could not proceed; some unseen barrier was stopping me. Fear started to swell up again, turning round although not able to see anything, I knew evil was most certainly there. It was almost a relief then when the creatures with the box appeared; if you can understand that. They were after me again. Setting off running once more I ran past the boy nailed to the tree; he was screaming for me to help him, every part of my body was telling me to stop to help him, but the fear I had for the creatures with box kept me racing on.

I found myself running down a street, my legs once more like lumps of lead the box carriers were catching me. I ran into this house, there were six people in the room all dressed in black and all with long white faces. I ran to a door, it opened onto a staircase. I knew there was evil up there, but the creatures with the box were gaining on me, I was terrified, I could hardly move, they were gaining.

No, no, no – not again – please God, no.

The Man

The man sat in the corner seat of the train; he was staring out of the window. He was about thirty-five, clean-shaven, and wore smart clothes. He looked very similar to a lot of people who have to catch trains, for whatever reason. The platform was extremely busy with people hurrying to get seats or indeed just trying to catch the train before it left the station. The man never took his eyes from the window for one second.

The train pulled sluggishly out of the station, and as if a signal had been given, people began to move. Some got papers out, some got mobile phones out, the ones who had been fortunate to get seats got flasks out. The man never took his eyes from the window, even though the scenery had now changed from platform to industrial scene. The industrial scene soon gave way to a more pleasant view, green patches and fewer buildings. This scene in turn quickly turned into open countryside with cows and sheep in the fields. The man still never took his eyes from the window, totally oblivious to the din around him.

The train had one stop and that was now approaching. The people who were alighting were now fumbling with papers, phones, flasks and things. Others were looking round ready to grab any vacated seats. As the train slowed and drew into the station, the man kept his eyes to the window. People were fighting to get off; people were fighting to get on. The platform was a hive of activity, the expression on the man's face never changed.

Forty minutes later the train drew into Noxford, and the same battle began again, with everyone wanting to be the first off to grab the taxis and buses. The man sat perfectly still, his eyes still focussed out of the window. It was not until the platform was clear that the man stood up, picked up his small briefcase and headed for the platform. He walked slowly up to the ticket collector, handed over his ticket, and walked down the station concourse and out into the city. He turned right and headed towards the bus station. He passed three shops – a florist, newsagents and chemists, at each one he stopped and stared for a few minutes through the windows. He didn't enter any of the shops.

When he arrived at the bus station, the bus for Wetherton was just pulling in. He got on, paid his fare, sat down, and immediately turned and stared out of the window. This being a rural bus, there was little activity. When the man saw the sign for Wetherton approaching, he stood up and made his way to the door. The bus stopped and he alighted. When he got to his house, he opened the door went into his kitchen and made himself a pot of tea. He then went back into his room, pulled a chair up to the window and whilst sipping his tea, looked out over the field.

Shortly after, he slowly turned to his briefcase and clicked the catches with his two thumbs. The lid seemed to hesitate and then it sprung open. The man then stared into the case. The knife stared back at him, the blade covered in blood. The man's eyes then slowly traversed to the newspaper cutting on the table at the side of the case. He read it for the fiftieth time.

The drunken driver of a stolen car, who knocked down and killed a newly married teacher at Wetherton three years ago, was released from prison after serving just three of the five years he received. He has never showed any remorse. This paper has received many protests about the apparent lack of justice.

He didn't read any more of the whole page devoted to the case, he walked over and looked longingly at the photograph of a beautiful young woman on the shelf. He then went back to his seat by the window, took a capsule out of a box on the table, put it in his mouth and swallowed it. He then stared out of the window, and never looked back.

He would not have heard the police car siren in the distance.

"David Kaprun, Doctor David Kaprun?" The man looked up recognising that it was his name being called, and stepped slowly forward.

"Don't look so worried, place your right thumb on this pad," instructed the interviewer behind the desk. The screens burst into life, but the images went far too fast for David to follow. The interviewer seemed to have no problem though. When the screens faded he said, "Well now, not bad at all, let's see then – ten to twenty: very talented pupil, worked hard at school, a good tenor, in the local choir; doing really well at music particularly violin. Twenty: went to medical college, passed final examinations with honours. Played and sang in local orchestra and choral society when work permitted. Thirty: now a consultant cardiologist at the district general hospital. Well, so far quite brilliant."

The interviewer then looked up at the man, and continued, "Thirty-one: married Lorna, the young lady you met at college. You bought a cottage in the country at Wetherton, and you were married there. Shortly after you were married, Lorna was knocked down by a drunken driver; he was speeding through the village in a stolen car after committing a robbery. Lorna died the next day. I see she was returning from the village hall where she had been instructing the girl guides in first aid."

The interviewer expressed no emotion whatsoever as he relayed these details.

"The driver is sent to prison. Let's see now, you leave the hospital and set up in general practice in the village. You are still living in the same cottage. Now you find out the driver of the car has been released from prison early. You do some investigating and find out where he is living. You take a knife and kill him – then return home, and take your own life, hoping to be reunited with Lorna. Anything important I have missed?" said the interviewer.

"No, that seems about right," said David, clearly upset at having to listen to these details. "What happens now?"

"Well, I cannot discuss details with you, I just award the entry level. You then go to that desk over there for further discussion before entry. I am awarding you level three."

David Kaprun looked puzzled.

"Don't look worried, that's quite good, you are the same level as Lorna." For the first time the interviewer allowed himself a brief smile.

David was directed to another gentleman, who was sat behind yet another desk. He was invited to sit down, and then asked if he had any questions.

"Well I cannot deny I am very worried about these three things: hating the man who killed my Lorna; killing him; then taking my own life. Three things I had been taught were wrong and unacceptable."

"Well I think you did rather well, and I fully agree with the award of three. That may amaze you. I considered you were human and acted in a human way – you were not a saint. You just cannot act like saints when you are not saints. You are told to love everyone, how can you be expected to love everybody? It is clearly silly. You should be kind and charitable, and fair to all, and you were. Yes, and more so than most. What you did deserves praise not condemnation. You killed the man who took her life, out of love for her. In doing that act which took courage, you undoubtedly spared other innocents from being killed by him. Have no doubt about it, and we know he would have killed again. If you had delayed in taking your own life for ten minutes, you would have been arrested, and tried for murder. You would have received a longer sentence than the evil one who took your wife's life. Don't worry, we know what is going on – even if we can't interfere."

"But I took another man's life."

"Well yes okay, and normally that is pretty serious stuff, but Lorna's life was worth a thousand of his. He had been involved in a lifetime of crime and violence. You did your society a big favour. Lorna and you were a perfect couple, giving generously to the community; you did nothing to invite this situation. Why in heavens name should you be punished for it? We like to let common sense prevail."

"Does everyone have to see you?"

"Not me personally. I have many colleagues who deal with entries; they all come through here though, this is the only point of entry."

"Do you know everything about people who come through here?"

"We are never fooled David, we know everything, and we are not allowed to make mistakes. The boss keeps a close eye on us, and sometimes we can be very harsh. Many get level two and below – that is very sad.

"By the way you have only just missed the man who killed your Lorna, the smirking fool – he still doesn't show any sign of remorse. He was a career criminal; theft, drugs, cars, assault; he would never have changed. Still we will have the last laugh. He was awarded a one minus that's the lowest you can get; he won't be smirking when he finds out what one minus means – okay then my friend off to the reunion room with you, about ten yards on the right – Lorna is expecting you. I will see you around."

A few seconds later David was in the arms of Lorna. Their life together was about to re-start.

The Strange Case of Richard Chartaris.

It was his son, a serving police officer, who brought the small article along to his father's home whilst on a casual visit. He thought it might be interesting. Richard Chartaris had recently retired from work, and was busy in his retirement. He could always find plenty to do around the house, and loved walking his dog, in fact he didn't know how he ever had the time to work. What was lacking though was the unpredictable event – that sudden excitement, the adrenaline rush.

His son had brought the article from the police station, it had appeared in a Home Office circular. It was only a few lines long and tucked away at the bottom of a page. It asked for mature and active ex-police or military personnel, to assist with interesting developments. The applicants had to be totally honest, fit, and willing to abide by the Official Secrets Act. Interviews were being held locally. It did not give any details about the work, how many people were wanted, or of what age or gender.

Richard read the article a few times and discussed with his son what the article could be about. They had no idea. He of course had the delusion of an 007-type job, but this was clearly preposterous. After discussing the article with his wife, who was in agreement with his applying (no doubt to get him out from the house more, she being of the opinion that he had retired too early), Richard rang the number. He was put through to an automatic answering machine, which was clearly set up to eliminate anyone not astute very speedily.

He was a little surprised therefore to find himself being supplied with another number to ring. The second call was answered by a human voice, and after a few questions he was invited to attend for a talk. Three days later Richard Chartaris found himself in a grubby street in the city. Looking at the signs and numbers he eventually found the sign he wanted: *The British Textile Development Company*. The grimy sign hung over an equally grimy entrance, not at all what he was expecting. Richard entered a little apprehensively, and introduced himself to the young lady at the desk. "Ah, Mr Chartaris, we are expecting you, please take a seat."

Richard was trying to look interested in a book about British tweeds when a very attractive young lady was ushered out of an adjoining room, and he was invited in.

"Richard Chartaris? – please sit down, don't be intimidated by these gentlemen, they are just observers. I am Colonel Crosby, the only military man here. These gentlemen are civilians; you may get to be acquainted with them later, but for now you will speak to me only. We already know a great deal about you, indeed you would be alarmed if you knew just how much, however I can assure you if you are not the person we are looking for, all those details will be destroyed."

Colonel Crosby then proceeded to grill Richard about all aspects of his life, and his working experience. He frequently looked at his monitor screen which Richard could not see. After about ten minutes, Richard interrupted:

"Colonel I am no longer in the forces, or even working. I am not prepared to be grilled anymore, please tell me what this is about or I will leave right now." The Colonel smiled and looked at his colleagues who were also now smiling.

"Mr Chartaris, your intervention came a lot quicker than we expected, that is very good, we can now proceed and tell you a little of what this is about. Before we go into detail we must ask you if you are willing to get your eyes sorted out. This is mandatory and you have nothing to lose. If we decide you are the man we want, you must have better sight – no spectacles. You will realise why later. We can offer you the best laser correction treatment free. Are you prepared to have the treatment, and to sign the Official Secrets Act? I must tell you now, no one else must know what is involved here; this is top secret work, and you will soon understand why."

Richard was totally intrigued by what he had heard and desperately wanted to hear more, He agreed to sign the form. With regard to his eyes, he had been considering having laser correction for some time, now he could have it free!

"Richard, I will now introduce my colleagues. These gentlemen are government men, Professor Ross, Doctor Grainger, and Professor Gibson. Doctor Grainger studies textiles; our professors are research scientists. In a few days if your eyes are okay and you want to proceed, we will be in a position to give you a demonstration and tell you some more details. Now if you wish we can do the physical check."

Richard passed the physical examination without any problems, and returned home with his head buzzing. Would they offer him a position? What on earth could it all be about? Richard was restless as he lay in bed. It was not anything to do with the laser treatment due the next morning, it was the intrigue created by his meeting with Colonel Crosby. What on earth could the demonstration be about? What had textiles to do with anything? Why should they be interested in him? Surely there must be an immense supply of intelligent fit young soldiers and police personnel who could fit their requirement? What was going on? Was he doing the right thing?

Richard had had an interesting life. He had though always found things difficult when others seemed to be cruising. He certainly was not an academic. He had obtained officer status while with Special Branch, attached to the police, but even then not at a high level. Richard was indeed pretty ordinary. The next morning a tired Richard presented himself at the private eye-clinic. It was soon established that the small errors in his vision were caused by the normal ageing process, and could be easily corrected. The specialist assured him that he would be able to dispense with his glasses. The first eye would be done that morning, if all was well the remaining one a week later. Richard was in for another restless night, but once again it was nothing to do with his eyes. The procedure had been quick painless and successful.

"We understand you are a linguist, Richard? You speak French, German and Spanish?"

"No," responded Richard, "you have bad information there."

Richard was back in the Textile Development Company office. Colonel Crosby was looking at some papers.

"Let's see then, final school report: 'speaks French fluently'. And here: 'attended college in Germany for a considerable time'. Did they speak English just for you?"

"You seem to have been digging up information on me."

"You wouldn't believe what we know about you Richard."

"Well, okay, I didn't mention a few things because they didn't seem as if they would have any bearing on the reason I was here. None of what you mentioned is any big deal, how can these things affect anything?" retorted Richard, clearly a little agitated.

"Well maybe they won't, but they could. Even at this stage we are not sure where we are heading, we really do need as much information as possible. I will now tell you what impresses us. You held a rank with the security services. Although you deny it, we know you are a polyglot. You also have an unblemished military record, and we are sure we can trust you. We have to be very careful here, but we have decided to go ahead with our demonstration. Only one other person has seen this demonstration, and has joined us. If after seeing it you decide not to join us, then that will put us in a difficult position. I must tell you now if that happens, and subsequently you break your security vow – well I do not think I need to spell that out. Now please come with me."

The Colonel and Richard went through to a back room that resembled a small laboratory. The two Professors and the Doctor were already there and greeted Richard as he entered. Doctor Grainger turned to Richard.

"Mr Chartaris, what you are about to see you will find extremely difficult to understand. We realise how important it is for you to know what this is about. Equally we need to know if you are able to continue with our experiment. We have been informed that your eye treatment was totally successful. You can of course continue your treatment whether or not you decide to stay with us. You can wear your spectacles for our demonstration if you wish. I must tell you there is no danger in what you are about to see, so please don't feel anxious. Are we ready gentleman?"

Richard was now glancing round the room, in the centre was a table about five feet long, it was covered by a glass frame and had what appeared to be a strip light tube at the top. There was a cable running to a small machine and some monitoring equipment. The lights were dimmed and Richard could hear a small humming sound. The strip light above the frame began to illuminate.

"Richard, look closely and describe what you see."

At first he could not see anything. His eyes scanned the enclosure which was now illuminated with a strange glow. Then he saw it slowly starting to appear.

"I see you have spotted it. Will you describe it please."

"What I see is some kind of material, maybe metallic, but only thin. It is about two feet long and one foot wide. I cannot describe the colour it seems to be scintillating – but not in a random way. It certainly seems strange. What is it?"

"Okay," the Colonel interrupted, "keep watching, we are going to remove it."

The cover was raised at the side and the object removed.

"Hold your arm out Richard. Don't be alarmed, there is no problem."

The object was placed across his arm, and the colonel said, "Okay gentlemen, switch off." The light in the frame on the table slowly went out, the humming sound stopped also. The room was lit by normal lighting.

"Now what do you see?"

The two professors, Doctor Grainger, and the colonel all stood round Richard. He was looking down at his arm, his mouth open and clearly unable to speak.

"Come on man," said Professor Gibson. "Describe what you see."

"But I can't," mumbled Richard. "I can't, my arm has disappeared."

"I can assure you your arm certainly has not disappeared," said Professor Gibson. "You just cannot see it, it is covered by our piece of material that is all, and our material just happens to be invisible."

The colonel turned to Professor Ross, who until now had been quiet.

"Richard," said the professor, "I will now attempt to explain things to you. I have been involved with the theoretical side of things here – my two colleagues are the practical men. Colonel Crosby is in charge of the whole thing but has no specific knowledge about our material, other than knowing what it can do. Firstly, just a little about colour theory. We know you have studied this Richard, but please bear with me. Colour is only reflected light, if a colour appears white it is reflecting red, green and blue light, which are the primary colours. If it appears green it is absorbing red and blue and reflecting green. If it appears blue it is absorbing red and green and reflecting blue. Objects are not really any colour, they only appear coloured if there is light to reflect. Articles appear black because they absorb all light, and reflect none. It follows then if there is no light, there is no colour.

"This is only basic of course, there is no need to go into the various tints and hues, which are a consequence of different conditions. So we have a situation of reflection and absorption. Now think about this Richard: what would we have if we could develop a neutral, a device or material that neither absorbed nor reflected light? I think you are beginning to understand Richard.

In fact we would have a material that is under all normal circumstances invisible. Scientists have been working on this since the Second World War. Forget all that HG Wells rubbish, it is not possible – nor will it ever be possible – to make a person invisible. However we have found out how to make the material that if placed over a person would render that person invisible. That is what this is all about. We want you to test it for us."

"But how would I be able to see it?" said a shaken Richard.

"Yes, okay, that is the really clever bit. Theory and practice had to come together for that part. Clearly, without being able to see the material, we could not work it, or indeed develop it. This proved to be the hardest part for us and took most of our development work. Just let us consider the electromagnetic spectrum for a moment. Most people will know the range: cosmic rays, gamma, x-rays, ultra violet, then visible rays, on to infra red, microwave, radio and television. In actual fact there is a limitless range of possible frequencies. We managed with the aid of filters to isolate the small frequency band that would cause our material to scintillate – in fact Richard your description was spot on. This is in actual fact one of the most closely guarded secret of all times. It can only be described as a miracle that we happened to stumble across it. But you need not worry yourself about that my friend. You are going to be our guinea pig. Now you know what this is about are you going to join us?"

Richard, although clearly shaken by what he had been told and seen, replied with a croaky voice, "Yes." Richard was trying to come to terms with the implications of what he had just seen and heard. The colonel came over and shook his hand.

"Welcome to the team my friend, we have a great deal more to explain, but first we have something really interesting to show you."

Doctor Grainger interrupted Colonel Crosby at this point. "I think Richard could do with a break now. I will tell him a bit more about our involvement before we proceed further with our demonstration."

"Yes, that's not a bad idea. Let's have some coffee and talk a while," said the colonel.

Doctor Grainger continued, "You need to know that we are only a small part of this thing, the development has taken place over a long period and involved many scientists and textile experts. We have now been split into four regions for testing purposes. Two people have been picked for each region. All tests will be done in this country, but obviously if things turn out correctly, future operations abroad will be a distinct possibility."

"There were initially 180 applicants for the eight places. Most failed at first contact, most of the remainder failed at the second interview or because our investigations revealed things that were unacceptable. A small number backed out after seeing our first demonstration. It was decided that this project would be left under overall control of the military, hence Colonel Crosby's involvement. The top ranking police officers in each region will be involved, before operations start.

"No other country is involved at the present, although the USA is aware of the project, they have not had the success we have, and we are not about to share it at this stage. We have here a tremendous project, which demands great responsibility and control. We are fully aware of the potential for evil if this should get in the wrong hands. We of course have certain safety features operating in the project, but most responsibility will rest with our selected eight candidates. The regions will not overlap so you will not encounter selected colleagues from other areas. You will be working this area with another person but mostly you will be working separately to start with. Your partner is a young lady, one Lucinda Forbes-Brown. You have already seen her, we understand."

"Was she the young lady leaving here when I first came for interview?"

"Yes that was her – eminently suitable, but more of that later." Doctor Grainger now stood up. "There is much more to tell you Richard, but we will wait while you and Lucinda can get here together, and then we can have a question and answer time. But now take a look at this."

Doctor Grainger produced a small bag and invited Richard to inspect it.

"Look inside," said Professor Ross.

"Okay, it's just an empty shoulder bag," replied Richard.

"Right, now watch carefully …. Can we have the illuminator again please?" The humming sound started again and Richard was led to the table.

"Now what do you see? Go on then, remove them." Richard removed two garments from the bag, which had now become visible to him. One resembled a large shawl, and the other a body suit. "We would like you to try these garments on now. You can do it with the illuminator on, however you will need to become expert at this because in future you will need to get these things on quickly without being able to see them. It will in fact be just like getting dressed in total darkness. The shawl has been designed for quick use, you can easily slip it over your existing clothing, it covers completely down to the floor, you will find you can see and breathe through the material perfectly well."

Richard pulled the shawl over himself.

"Switch off please." When the doctor stood back, Richard had become totally invisible. The four men laughed out loud at the sight of Richard removing the shawl, he could obviously feel it, but it was now of course completely invisible. More laughter followed as Richard slowly came back into view.

"Please excuse our laughter Richard," said Doctor Grainger. "But remember we are only human and this sure looks funny."

"It's okay," mumbled Richard. "I suppose it must look funny."

"We will leave you for a few minutes now," the doctor replied as once more he switched on the illuminator. "The garment you will try now is the body suit, this has been designed for all normal use. It is skin-tight covering all the body. It is also tight around the face – hence the reason for no spectacles. It is not claustrophobic. The texture inside is soft and comfortable, it has been designed to be worn next to the skin. It is warm in cold weather and cool in warm weather. You will have perfect vision, and normal breathing. Now, take everything off, on with the suit, and when you are ready, turn off this switch and knock at that door. We will not embarrass you by staying here while you change."

About five minutes later Richard knocked at the door, and the four gentlemen re-entered, Richard of course was nowhere to be seen. After about a minute Professor Ross spoke,

"So there you are Richard! Behind the table in the far corner."

"How the hell did you know that? This suit is supposed to make me invisible, and I have taken every garment off," came the voice from the corner.

"It is totally invisible my friend. There is just another small matter that we forgot to tell you about."

Professor's Ross and Gibson and Doctor Grainger were leaving. Their job was now over and they were returning to base. It had been their function to assist in the selection, and to demonstrate and explain as much as possible about the project. Richard could not fault them on anything. The few remaining things could be handled adequately by Colonel Crosby. Richard was genuinely sorry to see them go. They were thoroughly nice gentlemen in his opinion, and reminded him of some of his service colleagues of many years ago. He was happy that they had chosen him, although still somewhat surprised.

The next meeting was just for two. Colonel Crosby was to tell Richard about his intended partner, who was to arrive later that morning. Lucinda Forbes-Brown was indeed a privileged young lady. It would be correct to say in the true sense of the word that she had never worked. Lucy, as she was sometimes called, had been born into a very rich land-owning English family. Her father was a Lord and moved in very high circles. Lucy had been educated privately at home by tutors. She was proficient at riding and other country pastimes including shooting. After her private tutorship she had attended Oxford and taken a double first in English Lit and Language. She attended the London College of Music as a post-graduate, and gained a Masters. She was clearly a very clever lady. She also represented England in the Biathlon, being a very competent skier as well as a shot. Martial arts had not escaped her; she held a black belt. It may be said that a privileged life makes these things possible, but it cannot be denied she was one heck of a talented thirty-year-old. She had also been endowed with the body and looks to complement her abilities.

The four gentlemen who interviewed Lucinda had no intention at first of selecting her. In fact the day Richard saw Lucinda leaving the textiles office, she was convinced she had been rejected. This was purely on the grounds of her age. It had been decided early on in the search for candidates that the choice would be for mature and experienced, rather than young and keen. It was only after Richard's interview that they began to rethink. Although Richard and Lucinda's lifestyles had been totally different there was no denying the things they had in common. Lucinda was an accomplished writer, Richard also wrote. She was a composer of music, so was Richard. They were both studied martial arts. Lucinda admitted to speaking five languages fluently. Richard had at least some linguistic ability. They had no problem with her security rating, she came from a long line of military connections. It was decided to take a chance, they had much in common, and Richard could be a father figure. A short time later Lucinda arrived. The two gentlemen stood up to greet her.

"Lucinda Forbes-Brown, may I introduce Richard Chartaris," said the colonel.

"Hello Richard, I understand I have to thank you for my being here today." Richard had been rendered speechless by the gorgeous creature holding his hand, and was thinking what a crying shame it would be to render her invisible.

Richard managed a slightly delayed, "Pleased to meet you Lucinda."

"Right, just a few things then," said the colonel. You wanted to know how we knew where you were in the demo room, Richard. Take a look at this. He handed Richard a small device that resembled a thin torch.

"That, my friend, is an illuminator. It fits snugly in the body suit. When activated it emits a frequency outside the visible light spectrum which will locate another bodysuit or shawl. In your cases that will be each other. This device will only be used if you have strong reason to believe that you may be near each other, and no other communication is possible. Initially we think this will be unlikely. Please be aware when activated these unit consume a great deal of power. Five minutes is the maximum at the moment. So please remember, if you use it at all it must be replaced that same day."

"What's the range Colonel?" Lucinda just beat Richard to the question.

"You should obtain a reasonable scintillation up to about twenty five yards, day or night," replied the colonel. "Now, the most important thing, verbal communication. At all times when wearing the body suit, you will be in radio contact. You will wear an in-ear receiver, and a throat-microphone transmitter. The metal content of the fabric acts as the aerial. We will have contact with each other at all times. You will obviously be careful when using this equipment. The microphone is very sensitive, but be careful you are not overheard. In emergencies if you use the shawl, we suggest you fit your radio as soon as possible. It is essential that we have contact with you when you are, shall we say, incognito." The colonel then smiled and said, "Anyone want to back out? Okay then let's have your questions"

It was Lucy who spoke first. "Well I suppose we will both have questions to ask, now we have had time to think about things. I don't know about you Richard, but things have gone a bit too fast for me. So much has been explained about our garments and equipment that the whole reason for being here has passed me by."

"I totally agree," replied Richard. "So if I may ask the first question, colonel, what exactly are we going to be expected to do, and with what authority?"

"Right, that's a fair question and totally expected. To be honest we are not fully sure just what you will do. You were both chosen because we believe you will be responsible, discrete and sensible. Remember please that this is very much an experiment, you two and the ones in the other areas will very much determine the way the whole show goes. There are bound to be difficulties, we have all to remember that. We are not exempt from human rights issues, or from the constraints of political correctness. You will therefore have to act with the utmost discretion at all times. We are of course aware that although we think we have chosen well, you two are only human, and you may be tempted to use your new found abilities for some selfish reason. We trust you to act with decency and respect accordingly.

"Where do we see this thing leading? Well initially you will be working separately although you will be in radio contact. We want to know how you can help the authorities and law enforcers. We must stress we do not want you to jump in unilaterally to sort problems out which you may encounter, although you may find it tempting. No one will be able to stop you acting the way you decide, or even make you maintain radio contact at all times, it will be very much up to you."

"Why are we to work alone?" said Lucinda.

"The reason you will not be together to start with is purely because together you may be tempted to get into situations you would be better out of. Individually you will be more efficient to start with. Depending on how things work out will determine when we send you out together."

Richard interrupted. "Colonel, what authority will we be working with?"

"Another good question Richard. You will both go before a magistrate and be sworn in as government officials. This will give you basically the same powers of a police officer. We need you both to be legal."

Lucinda was ready with the next question. "Colonel, Richard and I have illuminators, will you have one?"

"No I will have contact by radio only," replied the colonel.

"Lucinda will be able to locate me, and I her," said Richard, and I can appreciate the advantage of this. Will anyone else be able to detect us? I know for instance that some people are known to be able to detect other's presence in a totally dark room."

The colonel thought for a few seconds before answering.

"Richard we have to be honest here. There is a possibility that your presence, even when totally invisible, could be detected. This is of course besides giving yourselves away by contact or noise. It seems there are probably two in every hundred who have this ability, and we don't know how it works, but it does. Some children, especially before puberty, also have this ability. We know however that animals, particularly dogs, would have no difficulty detecting someone in a darkened room, but this is down to smell only. The body suits that you and Lucinda will be wearing have been designed not to emit any body odours. We are convinced that your own dogs will not be aware of your presence.

"If you are ever in a situation where someone appears to be aware of you, we trust you will be able to deal with it. Remember they will never be able to see you, so this is very unlikely. But avoid busy places, people could bump into you. Do not use radios where you can be heard. Avoid heavy breathing when near to people. You have a lot to contend with, and you will not find it easy at first."

Lucinda and Richard exchanged glances but no more questions were forthcoming.

"Okay," said the colonel "That seems to be it. Richard, you have your other eye done tomorrow, so all being well we will soon be ready for our first trial. I suggest in the next few days you have lots of practice with your body suits."

As they were leaving the textile offices Lucinda turned to Richard with a worried look.

"Can I come round to your place before our first outing, Richard? I would like to meet your wife, and also we could possibly do some practice together. I would like to talk to you also; there are a few things that are troubling me."

It was mid morning three days later when Lucinda arrived at Richard's home. She was taken through to the lounge and introduced to Richard's wife Susan as Lucy. The two ladies spent some time talking, Susan was explaining about Richard's previous work with the security services, and the fact that she knew better than to ask him about it. She told Lucy that she had no idea what was going on but she hoped Richard would manage to keep her out of trouble. Lucy then explained that she had some problems with regards to the job and needed to speak to Richard.

"It really is no trouble, believe me, I am used to people calling all the time. I have to go out anyway so I will leave you to it. Richard will show you round and make you coffee," Susan said. She gave Lucy a peck on the cheek then went into the next room where Richard was just making coffee.

"I won't stay for coffee. I'll get straight off love. See you this afternoon." They kissed and Susan left.

"How did your eye treatment go, Richard?" Lucy asked when Susan had left.

"Fine thanks, no problem, it really does make an amazing difference, should have had it done before, but I have saved a few bob waiting," he said smiling. "I think it costs about two thousand pounds to have both eyes done. I will have to get some results now, they will expect it after forking that money out."

"Richard, that's why I came to see you. I am scared stiff about going out tomorrow. I just don't know what I am going to do, or indeed what I am expected to do. I have absolutely no experience of police work or indeed dealing with the public. If I was with you I would be okay, but on my own?"

"Look, you are going to be fine, just stroll round, keep your eyes open, and don't get involved in anything. You have radio contact and I have no doubt the colonel will be supporting you. He knows full well how you will be feeling and remember, he picked you because he had confidence in you. Now stop worrying about it and let's try our suits and see who's quickest. It may be important in future for us to be able to do this very speedily."

Richard turned around to get his pack, and when he turned back Lucy had disappeared. It was only when he saw garments appearing on the chair at the other side of the room that realised what was happening. Lucy must have had her shawl at the ready and quickly draped it over herself. She was now putting her body suit on under the shawl, and so was completely invisible to Richard. It was only then that Richard fully appreciated the importance of the position he and Lucy would be in. He had no idea whatsoever where she was.

"I am here, just to the side of you Richard," said Lucy. "Now get your suit on and don't forget your shawl first." The next hour was spent changing in and out of their body suits. Lucy was the quickest, but not by much. Whilst they were having coffee earlier on, the family dog, a Yorkshire Terrier, had been in the room. 'Tinks' had quickly made friends with Lucy and was soon on her knee. Before they tried their suits, the little terrier had been put in the garden, and was happily snoozing on the lawn.

"Will you put your clothes back on Lucy and bring the dog back in, I want to see if she reacts to me at all."

"Okay, just give me a few minutes, it takes longer this way." Richard smiled to see Lucy's clothes disappearing from the chair, and after a couple of minutes she reappeared fully clothed. "Okay, I will bring her in now. Are you ready?"

"Yes anytime," said the voice from across the room. A few minutes later Tinks entered. She immediately put her head in the air and sniffed. Her eyes scanned the room. Lucy was watching closely. This could be very important.

Richard was also watching and being careful not to breathe loudly or move. The dog looked straight at Richard and started walking towards him. Richard was thinking at this time about the smelling ability of Yorkshire terriers. Perhaps any other dog would not have detected him. This would have to be reported straight to the colonel. About a yard from Richard, she stopped, looked straight at him, then turned away and walked back out to her spot in the garden. Lucy closed the door and came back into the room.

"What on earth did you think of that?" she asked.

Richard's garments were now disappearing one by one from the chair.

"I really don't know. I was quite worried for a minute, if she had detected me that could have been disastrous. She certainly was aware of something. The strange thing is the nearer she got to me the less she was interested. If she had realised I was there she would have gone mad." Tinks was then let back in and did indeed make a fuss, jumping all over Richard in her usual way.

Lucy left mid-afternoon after some more discussion, and was in a more confident mind as she drove home.

Sleep didn't come easily for Richard that evening. Something was not quite right, and he was going over everything from the start trying to nail it. Why should they have been told about being discreet, about political correctness and sticking to normal guidelines? Then it clicked, it would of course be impossible to maintain these standards and make any beneficial use out of their ability to become invisible. The colonel told them these things because he had to – he knew damn well that all would go out of the window when he and Lucinda were let loose, and he expected it. Why has it taken him so long to twig it? He bet Lucinda had caught on all right, hence her concern. Richard was now able to relax, and fell asleep wondering what the morrow would bring.

The transit van arrived at the textile offices at eight am. Lucinda and Richard were waiting. The colonel walked in, said a brief "Good morning folks" and handed out the radios.

"Get these on now before we leave, we will have a quick test, then we will be off." It was clearly the colonel's intention to get the show on the road without any more discussion or delay. "Initial communication at this stage will only be with me, I have contact with the relevant authorities, if necessary I can contact them instantly. However at this stage I hardly think it will be required. Okay, in the van."

The transit looked normal from the outside apart from a number of small aerials. Inside it was different; in the back were two partitioned cubicles, a central table and some electronic equipment.

"Right you two, pick a cubicle, into your body suits, then out into the big wide world. I am not telling you anything else; it's now up to you. I will drop you quite a long way apart. You will have three hours to start with, then I will rendezvous with you, and we can have some lunch. Don't forget: if in doubt talk to me. Okay, Lucinda. Out the back door."

The van had travelled about two hundred yards when the colonel called Lucinda, "How do you read? Over."

After a few seconds delay came the answer. "Loud and clear colonel, sorry about slight delay I was just passing someone."

"Okay well done, and good luck. Out."

About fifteen minutes later Richard was dropped off, and a final radio check was carried out between the three of them. The colonel headed back to base.

Richard soon realised his problem: he couldn't be seen by pedestrians or road traffic users. People were walking straight at him, he had to take speedy action on a number of occasions. He was actually struck a few times but nobody seemed to notice. He chose a quieter street and walked past the Girls Central High School. He was attracted to a group of girls inside the school boundary. He could hear a loud voice and someone crying. He realised it was a case of bullying. A tall, well-built girl was harassing a small tubby child wearing glasses. Her cronies were in attendance giving encouragement.

Why are there never any staff about when this kind of thing happens? thought Richard who hated bullying.

The victim was clearly distressed and pleading to be left alone. The larger girl was on a roll and being egged on, was not about to give up. She was now prodding the small girl and her name calling was getting worse. Nobody noticed the bully's face move the first time, but after she cried out they certainly noticed the second time. Her face now had two red blotches, one on each cheek.

"Who did that?" she screamed. It was certainly not the small tubby child she had her head down and was still crying. The bully's legs then shot out from under her and she landed with a thud on her bottom. Her legs then started shaking, revealing her underwear. By this time all the other girls were laughing at the bully, and asking her what was going on.

"I know what's going on, it's you lot ganging up on me." She was now the one distressed, and as she turned to walk away it seemed for all the world that someone had kicked her up her behind and she went sprawling on the ground. The young victim was now laughing as loud as the other girls were.

Richard was thinking he really should have done something to help as he walked away.

Lucy was now getting a little more confident. She had managed to avoid any contact with others, had been in touch with the colonel a couple of times, and was beginning to enjoy her unique situation. It's amazing what one sees when not occupied with one's business, instead of head down and get there as quick as possible, she thought as she sauntered along. This was how she came to see the mugger. He had grabbed a bag from an elderly lady, pushing her to the ground. His mistake was that he was now running towards Lucy.

The mugger did a spectacular headlong running dive to the pavement; he then lifted his head up and smashed it down into the ground with a thud. When he got up, he had his left hand on his face, and his right arm pushed up his back, with his wrist at a funny angle. He then limped back towards the old lady.

A policeman had now arrived on the scene, and witnesses explained the situation. The mugger was duly arrested.

During their lunch break the colonel said debriefing would come later. Consequently, nothing much was said about the morning activity. Lucy and

Richard were clearly wanting to get back on the streets. The rest of the day was virtually uneventful, and with our two adventurers now in their normal attire, the colonel called them into the office.

"Right, just two reports from the police in your areas. First a girl from Central High reported an assault and a policewoman attended. Witnesses quickly established that there had not been an assault, the girl in fact had had some kind of fit. She is to have medical treatment. Later, from your area Lucinda, a mugger apparently fell whilst running away from an assault on an elderly lady. He somehow sustained a badly broken nose and a dislocated right arm and wrist. He was a wanted man; the police are delighted to have him back. This is the kind of thing you two could have been assisting in if you had kept your eyes open. Okay, go and have your discussion, I know you will have lots to talk about. We will have another talk tomorrow when you are back down to earth".

As Richard and Lucy were walking out of the door, the colonel followed, patted them both on the back and said, "Well done, you two."

The bombshell struck early the next day. Richard and Lucy were summoned urgently into the office and told they had to hand in all their gear. The plug had apparently been pulled on the whole thing.

The scheme had been reviewed again at the highest level and it had been decided that as tempting as it was to continue – and there was no denying the value it could offer – that it would be prudent to abort the operation. The advantages in countering physical offences and fraud cases were perfectly obvious and if the system could just be used for crime fighting then there would have been no problems. The guys at the top though had been viewing the whole thing from a political viewpoint, and knew that their secrets couldn't be contained and eventually the whole thing would be out of hand. It was decided then to destroy all evidence and all material. Nothing could be reproduced without all the detailed papers written over many years, and these were the first things to go.

Everybody involved was devastated by the news, but all realised after some thought that this was the obvious way to go. It had been an amazing experience for those involved and although they were told not to discuss it with anyone, it was realised that if they did, no one would believe a word anyway. Soon nothing existed anymore to do with the programme. The USA had been informed at the highest level that it had all been a failure, not to waste their time, nothing could ever come of it. All involved personnel had been dispersed.

Well there it is, that's the story. Just one more thing though. Two of the people involved with the testing in the northern area of the country never reported back or returned their equipment. Nothing has been seen or heard from them. It seems that they just completely disappeared.

Back to the Beginning

The following is not a story as such, however it does tell a story. It seems a good way to end this little journey. The cover picture of this book is of an Orb Web spider which I took in my Garden. It is said there are more varieties of spider on earth than any other creature, and if you believe in evolution the spider has changed far less than any other creature. After the dog the spider is man's next best friend ...

Well here it is. How it all started – no scientific stuff. Easy to understand – just as it all happened. All your questions answered.

Once upon a time there was this little thingy in the water. It didn't really know why it was there, even where it was, or what it was. In fact it didn't know anything because it was inanimate. One night there was a big thunderstorm and a lot of lightning. After a particularly large flash of lightning the thingy twitched. Blimey, I twitched then, thought the thingy. For a long time it sat there thinking about the lightning and the day that it twitched. The thingy thought that if it tried very hard in might be able to split in two. It had no idea why it should try to do this, it was a pretty thick thingy (it didn't have any brain) anyway it decided to do it anyway. So it cleaved – and behold we then had two thingies.

After a long time the first thingy had an idea. It only knew one word "cleave" because it had already done that. So it thought maybe it could cleave again, but this time it decided to do it a little differently. It was you see a bit cleverer now. So it cleaved again, but this time it used the other thingy to cleave with. And lo and behold after some time a little thingy appeared on the scene.

I have to take you forward quite a long time now. A lot of cleaving had been going on. I think the thingies were actually starting to enjoy it, because there were now quite a lot of them. The first thingy had started to get hungry, (I think it was because of all the cleaving) so it started looking for sustenance, it didn't want to die because it wanted to stay around for a while to do a bit more cleaving. The only things it could find were lots of little thingies. The little thingies were starting to grow quite miraculously into bigger thingies; that is the ones that hadn't been, er – not "eaten" – they didn't have mouths or indeed anything come to that; now there's a point – how did they do the cleaving? Umm, oh well the little ones were disappearing and it was thought the big things were responsible seeing that there was no one else around.

Not surprisingly the little things thought they had better try to save themselves, they were disappearing too fast and they were thinking about survival of the species (clever little things weren't they?) One particular bright little thingy decided that if some sort of propulsion was possible maybe they could get away from the big things that were causing their problems.

I have to move forward quite a few years now. Wow what have we here? It's a little thingy with a bit sticking out of it. When the bit sticking out waggles the thingy moves forward, we have motion. The little thingy is now of course a big thingy and getting a bit cocky. It was fed up with all the water and wanted to try something else, so having gained some mobility, it headed for the beach. Now that was quite a smart move, but when it got there it had a few problems. Wiggling onto the sand it found itself in trouble. It didn't know about oxygen (not having much knowledge other than cleaving and growing a tail) and the poor little thingy couldn't breathe. I am in trouble now, thought the little thingy, and after all them years growing my tail. But just then a wave came and pulled the thingy back in the water. A big shiny globe had appeared in the sky and it seemed to be making the water move. (Good job for the thingy).

So it was back to the drawing board, our thingy was not about to give up because it quite liked the look of the beach. And so it came to pass that after many attempts and a very long time, things (there were more of them by now) found that they could survive on the beach, and they quite liked it. They were lying about in the sun with nobody to bother them, yes indeed, life was good.

Now we came to the first change of direction. Some of the things decided they wanted to explore but found it was a bit difficult, they had to wriggle to move and kept banging into things. It took a long time (a very long time) but our things grew legs, they knew that legs would make them mobile (their brains had been developing you see), but they knew they would still be banging into things. So the logical thing they thought was: let us grow some eyes – we will grow two, just in case we get something in one of them. Good thinking that, wasn't it? The other things had decided not to bother with legs, and they burrowed into the sand, (they obviously didn't want to get sunburnt).

After a long time (a very long time) the things that had gone into the ground kept popping up and catching the things with legs and eating them. They had grown mouths by now and liked to use them. We will now call the things with eyes and legs lizards, because they still enjoyed a swim in the water occasionally. The lizards didn't always see the ground dwellers – they were very cunning blighters and laid traps for them. The lizards also caught the ground dwellers on occasions too, and ate them. The ground dwellers didn't like this and decided to grow legs also, but thought: we will grow legs also but we will have lots of legs, four aren't a lot of good. And behold they grew lots of legs.

Some of the lizards decided the safest place would be in the very tall things that were springing up. They would be safe up there. One day one of the lizards decided he was fed up of climbing up and down the tall things to catch the things with hundreds of legs, he wanted to turn vegetarian. He had spied a bush lower down near the water with lots of bright red things on it – but how to get there? He decided he would glide down (quite logical thinking) But how would he glide? And behold time passed (a long time) and our lizard found himself with membranes between his legs. (He didn't know they were membranes of course he wasn't that bright). However the bush with the bright red things was still there so he launched himself into the air and glided down to the bush, were he partook of the fruit, and lo it was good.

'What an idiot," exclaimed his mate who was still sitting on the tall thing. "He's messed it up now – he can never return. I will do better than that."

And so it came to pass, some time later (a very long time later) the first lizard had returned to the ground and decided there was no future in gliding (it only being one way). But his mate had more patience, he stuck it out, and eventually grew membranes that moved, he could get down to the red things, and then by flapping his front legs get back to his tall thing again.

The one who returned to the ground was now a reptile, the things with lots of legs were insects, but – he; he was nearly a bird.

He was actually a bit premature thinking he was nearly a bird, but he was a flying lizard of the early Jurassic era and that surely wasn't bad. After all it had only taken about 150 million years since that first cleave, and four to five billion years since the earth was formed.

Meanwhile back in the water, things were moving on apace. The things there had really been at it with vigour – things were now everywhere in all the waters, and there was plenty of waters. They had also changed a bit over the years. You will be aware that they too learned to see – this was absolutely necessary for them, to know what was going on, and there was plenty going on apart from the cleaving. Some of the things – the ones who were lazy, just wanted to stay local, so they grew flat. This was quite bright thinking from them, because they could sink into the sand beneath the waters and hide from the nasty things. They just emerged for a quick snack then disappeared in the sand again.

Others were only very small so they travelled about in schools, thousands of them, they knew there was safety in numbers (they learnt that at school.) so they were able to travel far and wide in relative safety. Most of the things had just grown big and ugly, they had learned to move very fast and were not just after sustenance and cleaving, they wanted to kill everything – just because everything was there. This action by the large ugly things stirred the smaller things into action. They started to explore the possibilities of leaving the water and going on to land. They had seen the lovely beaches and tall things and fancied to give it a try. It has to be much safer, they thought.

They were not aware than many years ago (very many years) that things had already taken to the land. This however was different. This was an exodus on a massive scale. So it came to pass that things left the waters all around the Earth at the same time. The areas that they left the waters determined how they would grow. They had of course to adapt to their own locations. Some found themselves in warm places, some very hot and some very cold. They quickly (well not too quickly) changed from water creatures into land creatures. They grew coats of hair in chilly climes and fur coats in colder climes. Their body shapes changed also according to their location and requirements. Some liked the leaves, berries and fruit that were by now in abundance so much that they stopped eating their friends. At this time the land masses were all joined together and some of the more adventurous things (now called "creatures') decided to explore, and lo they roamed and adapted over all the lands.

We now have to return to see how our flying lizard is progressing. Well, he was enjoying life. He could keep out of the way. And he needed to! The thingy that decided to stay on the ground had changed into a monster, in fact a variety of monsters. They had gone in different directions according to their needs. The tall things, which our early land dwellers had encountered, had turned into magnificent trees. Because they were very tall trees some of the creatures grew long necks so they could get to the leaves and fruit. Others had grown large bodies with large heads full of vicious teeth and they attacked and ate anything.

We are now in the time of the dinosaurs. From that first thingy and that first cleave we now find we have a populated earth and sea, and attempts at conquering the skies. The creatures that stayed in the waters became fishes (mostly) of various kinds. The ones who left the waters went in different directions. Some of the early crawling things eventually became crocodiles. Some turned into turtles and tortoises, some into toothed flying reptiles, and some into dinosaurs both large and small. Trees had been developing as some pace, these started off as algae in the sea and were quite well established when the first thingy went ashore.

At the start of the Jurassic era insects were well established and developing nicely. The amount of insects about also encouraged the start of the insectivore line. Wasn't it all magical? We now had insects, some flying creatures, turtles and dinosaurs of various shapes and sizes. The climate had been good, and early flowers are starting to appear. Because of the warm climatic conditions warm-blooded creatures (the first mammals) are starting to develop, but all creatures are still egg layers. There had also been much raising and lowering of sea levels causing early land shaping.

One day one of the dinosaurs happened to be stretching up to a tree to eat a particularly nice looking fruit – when he exclaimed, "What is that thing?" He didn't know of course because he only had a small brain (he didn't need a big one) that what was heading straight for him was a giant meteor. It hit the poor creature right on his head; alas everything in the impact area was immediately eliminated. Because of the size of the impact, large parts of the ground were turned into dust and ash. This debris soon circled the Earth and blocked the sunlight. All life was soon extinguished on Earth (What a shame after all that time?) Well I will just clarify that last statement; all life could not possibly have been extinguished! Or clearly I wouldn't be here writing this.

It is thought that maybe seeds from early flowers and trees survived in the ground, Quite amazing that! It was a long time (a very long time). It seems also that the first thingy, that decided to go down into the ground all those years ago was not so daft.

(He must have thought: if a giant meteor ever hits the earth, I will be finished if I am not under the ground) anyway it came to pass that the thingy with many legs, under the ground did apparently survive. He wasn't too bothered about what he ate and the dinosaurs had been well cooked – so he partook of them and they were good, and lo he sat the cold spell out underground. He was well fed reasonable cosy and quite content.

I would just like to take you back to that first cleave and the first thingy, if you can remember that far back (a very long way).

It is important that you realise there was only one first cleave. Please try to grasp this fact – it is very important to the story. That first thingy was our ancestor. Yes all of us, every living thing. We are all related by that first cleave. If that thingy hadn't had the notion and indeed the lightning strike at that very moment, none of us would be here. It could never have happened again. That one instance when everything was just right for the cleave was truly a miracle.

It is not and never will be possible to create life from an inanimate object (although many have tried) I suppose some may disagree with this, but may I just say, when you kill a fly you are killing a relative. When you stand on an ant you are squashing a relative. I do not know you or anything about you, yet you are related to me. We are all related – truly all the same family. Mice and rats are used for experiments that will ultimately help we humans. This is because their DNA (building blocks of life) are nearly identical to ours. We are all every one of us a miracle. We just happened to take different paths.

Just prior to the meteor striking the Earth, the range and different sizes of creatures was quite amazing. The largest was probably the diplodocus, which it is thought weighed up to forty tons and was up to ninety feet long – truly a giant. The early mammals were very small and primitive, no bigger than rats. They tended to live in woodlands and it was these creatures that miraculously decided they would like to be warm blooded. Also being fed up of having their eggs eaten – they decided to give birth to live young, so they could look after their offspring a bit better. Another amazing development – warm blooded live bearers who suckled their young. These were truly our ancestors. It is thought that these early creatures may have been the ones who first stood on hind legs to reach up – possibly they were the line that started the grasping hand.

I would like to go forward now to a strange time in our history called the

Cambrian explosion. You will recall that after the meteor strike and total demise of the dinosaurs it was thought that only the underground dwellers could have survived. This would have been the end of us of course. Cleaving had been going on a very long time, and there was no way it could pick up from where it left off – or as we know start again. It seemed we were well and truly messed up. But we now know because of fossils that have been found that there was a parallel evolution-taking place. This line was of very small creatures – very small, so small in fact that they went unnoticed for a long time. How they survived is a total mystery, but it is to this line that we must give our thanks also.

This Cambrian explosion was truly amazing, placental animals had really got going and we began to see the start of modern animals appearing: elephants, rhinoceros, horses, pigs and cattle. All the giant reptiles had gone but turtles and tortoises abounded. This may surprise you but in the Cambrian explosion all the insect types which we have today were present. They may have changed slightly but no more groups have been formed. This is now perhaps the strangest thing of all. Fossils have been found that indicate at this time that primitive monkeys and gibbons were in Burma. Where did *they* come from? Oh well, it seems we are getting a little nearer to our true ancestors (or are we)?

About eleven million years ago land masses and oceans began to take on new shapes. Continents were being formed, seas were being created, and animals were being marooned in faraway places to their birth. Mount Everest was at one time beneath the waves (deep-sea fossils have been found near to the summit). Just prior to the ice age (Pleistocene), man-like apes were continuing to develop and thrive. These apes included not only the forest dwellers – but wait for it! Australopithecus - an ape-like creature who walked upright and ventured into open country. Well, think what you will now, but – what line did he come from? Anyway there he was; he found out that he could roam further and reach higher whilst on two legs. It is thought that grasping hands were developing nicely when he appeared, and he developed them a bit more.

During the ice ages sea levels rose and fell and new land appeared. Glaciers were also further shaping the land. Mountains and lakes continue to form. Lions were roaming the dales of Yorkshire where I live, and horses now roamed the land – very similar to present day horses. At the end of the ice age ten thousand years ago, the melting ice caused the sea levels to rise dramatically. The rising waters separated Britain from Europe. Temperatures rose much higher. In North Africa and the Middle East deserts begin to form. With the decrease of the ice and warmer summers, forests begin to spread all over Europe. Modern types of trees then started to appear.

Now we arrive at the Holocene period. Early man had learnt to domesticate animals and cultivate the land. He had obviously by now developed the skill that would set him apart from all other animals, the ability to kill from a distance. Only man among all of the entire animals in the world can do this. He started with rocks, throwing them. Then he started to shape them for cutting. Then the natural progression to attaching them to sticks (he had invented the spear). Soon after he was not only killing animals (for food and skins) but he was killing his fellow men. And that was the start – or maybe we could say the start of the end. From that first cleave man had developed into the ultimate killing machine.

A relatively recent United Nations report stated that it is known that man is responsible for the extinction of five hundred species of animals and maybe many more. Many glorious birds have disappeared never to return. The report also states that man has destroyed even more species of plants. Ours is most likely the only life anywhere, and it was a miracle that it ever started. The animals we have eliminated were our family. We have fished the seas till they are nearly empty, and now we bottom drag them for any other edible species that may have been missed. This action causes the death of thousands of tons of other sea creatures, which are just dumped back dead – as useless to man.

We continue to shoot birds for sport. We continue to hunt foxes, hares, badgers and now even polar bears among other animals for sport. (Some sport!). We are very quickly using up our supplies of fossil fuels, we have decimated our forests, we are surely destroying our eco-system. What then have we achieved? Our greatest achievement beyond any doubt is our ability to kill from a distance. And haven't we exploited that?

If we want an analogy for the time of life on Earth, we could use a day. We would actually have been around only for the last couple of seconds of those twenty-four hours. If we group together the sea monsters, the dinosaurs, meteor strikes, and the ice ages, we don't come even close to the destruction to life that humans have been responsible for in their short time on Earth. Human beings keep telling themselves how wonderful they are. But I wonder just how wonderful that first (thingy) all those years ago would think we have turned out if he could see the end product of what he started? I suspect he might have wished he never had that first twitch.

By the way, fossils have been found to cover the continuance of all species on Earth including most of the dinosaurs. The only transitional fossils that cannot be found are the ones linking the apes to humans. Strange isn't it?

www.ingramcontent.com/pod-product-compliance
Lightning Source LLC
Chambersburg PA
CBHW030527260626
47157CB00005B/1911